I0542737

MERCY, MERCY ME:

A Journey of a Madman in Love

TL DARWIN

Mercy, Mercy Me: A Journey of a Madman in Love

Copyright © 2007 by TL Darwin

All rights reserved. No part of this book may be reproduced or transmitted in any form or by any means without written permission of the author.

ISBN 978-0-6151-6684-1

Library of Congress Control Number: 2007941232

Dedicated to my sons, Octavius and Alexander, and my daughter Liliana, may your names be the bulk of your worries and concerns.

To my friend and confidant, Kathryn, whose faith, loyalty and belief makes mountains seemingly disappear. Thank you.

To my editor Lindsey Murdock, thank you for your guidance and entrepreneurial spirit, you're the best.

To all my loved ones who twinkle like stars trying to stay as bright as you can for as long as you could…as we all should. Thank you.

To every person in the world Living Dead Lost in Love… remember… Life is Love and Love is Life, both are eternal -- So are you!

From the very beginning I knew the devil well. My heart had been shown its deceitfully sweet ways. My mind formed, my actions shaped by a desire to win in love, introducing me to the essence of the creator. The two began to fight…leaving me lost and confused, desperately seeking someone, anyone to alleviate my pain.

So, the lies began, the day that damn doctor smacked me on my ass, and I have been screaming every since.

I remember almost the exact moment I knew something was wrong. The lump in my throat told it all and my desires were overwhelmingly clear. I had been bitten, but I didn't care. It didn't sting. It didn't swell. It was, well, delightful, as if I had fallen from on high, never touching the ground. I could fly…

It's funny how things work in the game of love. One minute you're supposedly madly in love with someone, the next it's okay, and then it's hell. I have learned through life experiences that this isn't love at all.

It is precisely what we have all labeled it as… "The Game."

The wonderful thing about discovery is once something is found, it is no longer lost, and being becomes. Love is. And he who learns this early on finds a true foundation based on a substance that is always forming, showing and growing.

All of this came flooding to me as I drove along, headed for nowhere. Reflecting back over my life in love made sense, but caused a shiver down my spine like an Alaskan sunrise.

And, I swear she had to be the best I have ever had, even to this day…

But, (you know there has to be a "but"), I never have professed to know much.

One thing I have learned -- life is all about the ride. Enjoyment has always been an option, an option seldom picked by many. Close your eyes, breathe deep and slow, on a journey we're about to go. Now…

Imagine Curves...

Look at that,
What a wonder to amaze,
Soft as silky sheets
Flowing softly down
Heavenly feel, warming glow
Touch so divine, cannot explain...but feel
One only knows that this is it,
Awesomely exploring, one step at a time,
Methodically understanding the task at hand,
She watches and waits with breath so slow
In, out, up, down
Trudge softly and listen well...
Choose wisely and hug those tight, tight curves

TL

igh school, I remember it like yesterday, the beginning of my senior year, beginning of love anew. I was use to roaming through the hallways before Chemistry class with my buddy, Alan, playing our game "Best Gentleman." We tried to find girls who were in our class, asked to carry their books and escorted them to their seats, finding as many as we could, trying to out do each other. It was a classic Tony and Alan case, too much testosterone in its purest form, driving two sports heads determined to prove which one was better than the other. In my mind, I knew it was me.

Rounding the corner while engaging in a serious debate with Alan on why the ladies preferred the likes of me, I soon discovered what it was like to be captivated, mesmerized and to have feelings of grandeur, to know what it was like to be with someone, to call them your own, to know discovering your high school sweetheart, my first vision of love...

"Come on dog, you know I'm the smooth one of the two. I can't help it that I got it like that, man. If you relax a bit, maybe I'll show you a thing or two. Just follow my lead, son," I said to Alan while giving him a little pat on the back.

"Brother please. You a Georgia boy. By the time I get anything from you it'll be time to consider retirement. Besides half the fun is in the chase. You need to stop trying to win'em anyway. Let's just play."

"I feel ya, but..."

Alan saw her too. Little did he know, I was playing for keeps and was bound and determined to get to her first. First impressions last a lifetime.

Full speed ahead, I ran up on her so fast, she must have thought I was insane. And I guess I was in some regards. But, I got her, and the day was a good day, the day Sam became mine, and I knew it, the very first moment I ever laid eyes on her.

"Hello. May I?" I said to her while gently wrapping her arm within my own and taking her books away from her. I couldn't stop looking in her eyes, which seemed to sparkle with words and magical places I had never been before and in which I always wanted to be.

"Why sure you can, handsome," she said softly with a bit of a giggle.

I looked over at Alan as we walked by and gave him the head-bop; just to let him know what I said earlier was proving itself to him as we strolled past.

"Punk," I heard him mutter jokingly under his breath.

Maybe, I thought, but this girl is fine, with her silky smooth skin, nice long reddish brown hair layered and falling over her face, revealing the thinness of her slender jaw-line and the succulent look of her lips, not to mention the way her figure resembled an hour glass wrapped in a golden blouse, standing on a fabulous pair of legs showcased underneath a black mini.

Sorry, Alan, you lose.

And the rest is history… ancient history it seems sometimes but not all the time, like now…

Flowing...

There you stand, eyes fixed on the object you love,
Thoughts proceeding words of splendor from above,
Heart racing, full of glee,
Body trembling from ecstasy,
It hits you and instantly you can tell,
This story you know oh so well,
Revelation, karmic bliss,
Unforgiving, shocking, a can't miss,
All of these things come to pass,
But all dissipate, they never last,
Instinctively you interrupt this flow,
A simple touch showed you so
A measurement unlike any other
One that is wanted and needed no further
Than the moment it occurs
Slowing, stopping, restarting, it blurs
From that moment forth things just aren't the same
The rules are broken, a different game
Smartly you search and search
Trying to equal this change with hurt
In the end you only find it to be true
Interaction is great between me and you...

TL

I can recall the essence of Sam and how much we clung to the newness of our found oneness. We had discovered this great secret about living only a relative few have found, the secret to lasting joy and happiness in being with one another.

"Sam, I don't quite know how I got through life without you," I said to her one day after finishing our last set of tennis practice. "I mean, my life was shitty before you came and made it okay." I held her around the waist as we walked from the court. "I didn't have any cares about anything besides sports. I just didn't," I continued.

"What about Alan?" she asked.

"Yeah, that's my man. He definitely made a difference, but he don't get me completely. We're cool and all but we're different too, you know?"

Having been through a struggle to just stay alive, Sam was a welcome relief for me. Life had dealt me some pretty rough cards, from the death of a mother who was strung out on drugs, making it hard to know who she was half the time, to having to work at a young age doing anything to keep food on the table for my mom and my three sisters, to a father of whom I knew but had never made a connection with, someone who I despised and who hated me equally for intruding on his life. I was forced to live with him because I had no other options, other than the foster-care system when my grandmother died four-months after my mother passed.

So here I was.

Life had sucked until she came.

I would have done anything just to see her smile.

She made me feel alive.

"Yeah, I understand Tony. I wish your life could have been different, but if it would have been, we would have never met, and I would never wish that," she said, leaning over and kissing me on my forehead. "Now let's go get ice-cream."

"Sure."

"Hey Tony, I have an idea. I've started this journal," Sam said to me one day in the hall between classes, handing me this shiny pink notebook with the first page filled with her beginning words of love.

"It is our journal of how we feel and see things around us. I call it our dream come true book," she happily exclaimed.

Here's the thing. I was a developing young man, with growing biceps and a very masculine physique, carrying around a pink notebook in which I was to indulge all of my private thoughts for the sake of us…I was game.

Alan found it hilarious; he also thought I was causing serious problems for the rest of the guys.

"Tony, man, what are you doing? You're taking this boyfriend thing to another level son" (The good 'ole 90's lingo). "God, you're making us have to step it up, son," he said.

"It's not like that, god, I am feeling this girl, and she just might be the one, son."

This brought a look of laughter, pain and constipation to his face, as he slumped back into his chair.

My man Alan and I were guys who liked to chase the girls, but we were also into school, both wanting to be engineers, both competing to do big things. This didn't fit into the plan, and it was definitely something we had never discussed.

It just wasn't possible.

"Tony, man, this is high school, son. You can't be serious...are you?"

"Dead as a doorknob serious, son. She is the one, god, never felt like this about nothing. Look at me, son. I open doors, carry her purse, play tennis, and I stopped playing football; come on now, god, how else or what else can I say to explain it. It's her, son. She's it. The one. The love of my life, god."

Sam and I were explorers.

We sought out life in love, not even knowing what we did.

We walked and talked, meditated, and grew close to each other from points un-experienced by most high school loves, forging paths into trust beyond the idea of merely just having someone. She came from a family of love. Her father was the first male she had ever loved, and he was practicality the frame of her decision- making in love. Her mom's warmth encouraged her to have sympathy for those who did not have the support of a family.

"Sam, I don't think I am going to go to college once I get done with high school. I am tired of this shit, tired of having to prove things to people because everybody thinks I am smart and they think I should or they're all just waiting for me to fail. I need to get out...to get away," I said to her one night as we sat on a hill looking into the city, after having a nasty argument with my father about the direction of my life after graduation.

She knew all about me. She knew I came from the depths of southern poverty, having to scrounge for money, food, clothes and a place to live, while keeping a thirst for knowledge and a desire to live. She knew I had witnessed violence of mass proportions. Social violence that had been physical, mental and emotional, seeing it used not only on and by others but having felt the wrath of violence being used against me also. It was a vicious cycle, producing victims against victims, making it hard for me to be real with anyone.

WACK!!

"Ahh, my arm, my arm!" I screamed, as I felt my left arm break, allowing the warmness of the tears to fall down my face like rain. As the throbbing ran up and down my arm with what seemed like the ferociousness of a billion fire ants, I braced myself for another blow.

"Shut-up, you little punk-bastard!" I heard from the dark-faced, angry man standing over me with a 2X4 in his right hand, as I lay on the cold; slab-cemented floor in the hallway of our project, crying in pain, but keeping the sobs low to not get hit again. "You're a little walking-dead punk, good for nothing but getting your ass beat!"

I could smell the words coming off of his cheap-gin-laced breath as he fired them down upon me - a victor over his spoils, his weapon now perched on his shoulder.

I remained tucked in the fetal position, praying he wouldn't touch my sisters and that my grandmother would wake up, until I heard him hit the floor in the other room, passed out from too much of a good thing...

She had heard the countless stories of trying to make it through another day. She knew I had lots to prove, with shoulders so weighed down by want and expectations that life seemed impossible sometimes. She knew.

"Tony, just follow your heart," she said, "I will always love you, no matter what you do."

"Really?" I asked, as the wind from the river whipped against my face.

"Really," she said, taking my hands in hers as we stared into the city at the twinkling lights.

My man, Alan, and I decided we wanted to start early on tuxedo shopping for the prom. Since we were both going to be on the court, we wanted to stand out.

"Man, I like the new Michael Jordan line of tux," Alan said as we browsed through the various styles adorning the racks of Men in Black.

"Forget Jordan, man, he's a bum," I said sarcastically. I was a die-hard Magic fan. "Now if they had the real MJ line, then I would consider it. What do you think of this Pierre Cardin?" I asked, sizing it up in the mirror. "I think I might have found mine, god," I said, eyeing what I thought was a masterpiece, a white tux with black lapels and a black cummerbund. "This is definitely me, especially with some white Stacy's."

"Son, I think we should both get that joint and definitely rock a pair of white Stacy Adams with it. And check it bro', my Pops has several canes we can pimp out, too."

Alan was pumped.

Being a dark skinned brother like me, standing about 6'1'' 185 pounds, and always carrying a brush to keep his waves up, Alan was already at the prom in his mind, surrounded by the ladies and the envy of the fellows, so I knew it had to be the one.

We made our purchase and were walking through the mall with Alan hawking and me in my own little fantasy world of life after high school, when we seemingly bumped into an exhibit of my fantasy coming to life, revealing itself three hundred feet in front of my eyes. Three men dressed in black and blue, looking like the guardians of a brave new world. I knew from the moment I saw them I was game. I was hooked.

"Slow down, god, what's up with you?" Alan asked, looking disturbed, as I sped up, hurrying toward the setup.

"Man, that's it," I said pointing at the men in blue, "that's what I want to do with my life, son, right there," I said, walking up to the men and leaving Alan behind.

I left the mall that day with more than what I went there for. Alan didn't have a clue what had taken place. He thought it was me being the spontaneous prankster and drama king I usually was. He didn't have a clue I had found the next phase of my life, quite different from our original plans. If he knew, he would have killed me.

Not only had I fallen head-over-hills, hard in-love with a girl from a game in high school, I now wanted to become a super-intense freak of destruction. I had lost my mind. I knew Alan would say, yell and beat this into me. So I said nothing. He just wouldn't understand.

I did tell Sam later that day after I got off from work.

"Sam, I have something to tell you," I said to her as we were out walking her St. Bernard, Nicky, through the park, with the sun rapidly setting behind us.

She slowed and looked at me with a look of fear and sadness.

"And it's not what you think," I said, immediately reading all over her face what she was conjuring in her heart. "I have decided what I want to do with my life. I am joining the Marines," I said, half expecting to hear her scream WHAT!

But she didn't.

"Tony, I think you'll be the baddest-fucking Marine I know, and you'll be mine," she said, bounding toward me, giving me a big bear-hug as she deep kissed me, making me feel connected to the slippery and erotic slither of her tongue dancing around and around inside my mouth. "I am so happy for you," she said as we came out of our trance in search of air.

"Thank you. I am so excited. We will be able to travel and see the world and I can go to school and get my degree after we get settled. It will be great!" I said, letting the words flow from my mind without a pause.

"We?" she asked, stepping back, looking at me with her head cocked slightly. Nicky began to tug her back toward her house.

"Sam, I love you, and I couldn't imagine you not sharing my life with me and me with you. I can't do this alone anymore. I don't want to do this alone anymore." I turned to face her as the sun began to set behind the thick cover of trees, Nicky looking up at me as if I was a nut.

We stood there for awhile watching the sun further descend behind our cover of greenery, my mind wondering if I had isolated yet another person, hacking off the delicate sweetness of love before it had a chance to take root and survive on its own...

"I know, Tony, but I want to go to school. I have always dreamt of being at college and

having that time in my life be a great thing. I
have to do that, but it doesn't mean we won't
be together. I just need to go away to school
for the experience it brings," she said, dropping her head, feeling my disappointment over-
take our conversation.

My heart dropped. I knew the truthfulness
behind those words, although I wished them
away. I wanted her all to myself, but I instantly knew how selfish of me it seemed. She
had rescued me from the depths of a living
hell, and all I wanted to do was show my appreciation for the rest of my life to her
alone.

"Tony, we will always be together. This is
just something we will have to figure out and
get through, me and you together, okay?" she
asked.

"Okay, but I don't like it," I growled,
biting her on her neck to break the negative
space that was to come between us.

I refused to let it be, I thought, as she
broke away from me and ran toward her house
with Nicky leading the way.

I gave chase, thinking she would forever be
my lady.

Sam and I both had been in relationships
with others before, me with girls that were
into the makeup and "becoming-a-woman now
scene" and her with guys who thought they were
men who knew how to treat a woman.

We could hardly contain ourselves from being overly physical. Sex was on our minds all
the time. Everyone seemed to be doing it, and
enjoying it.

One evening while having a Snickers ice-cream sundae at our favorite parlor, Sam dropped the question that had our insides tingling with anticipation, mindlessly running away with our thoughts.

"Tony, we have been seeing each other for a while now, right?" she asked.

"Yeah, we have, and I have been loving every moment, because our time together is running out," I said, thinking of my looming ship out date, the day I had to head down to Paris Island for boot camp and begin the fight for my manhood.

"Oh, Tony, you're being sensitive again, we still have a few months left before you and I leave. Besides, I was thinking maybe we should get a little closer, cause if your kisses are anything like the rest of your lovin', I can't wait out much longer," she said, running her hand under my shirt and rubbing my chest right as I put a spoonful of ice-cream in my mouth.

I almost choked, but I kept it together well enough to give a response.

"I am definitely feelin' that, boo," I said, cool, calm and collected.

But nothing could prepare me for my very first time with a girl on her very first time, built up through the imagination, recognition and recording by paper and pen. That journal. That "dream come true book," painting the way to heaven on Earth and magic under the sky, on a crisp October night, beginning the outlining of my masterpiece...And the rest is history, ancient history it seems sometimes, but not all the time, like now.

Reflections

Sometimes words paint a picture so clear to me,
In focus, full of life for all to hear and see,
Placing you in magnificent view,
Sparkling and shining from the morning dew,
Listen to the beauty at hand,
Like flying high over the land…
Somewhere deep inside, you swell,
Bubbling over, I sure can tell,
Wonderment and joy fills the air,
From the touch and smell of your hair,
Visualizations seem so real and true,
Whenever I'm with you…

TL

fter the night the Earth seemed to shake and the sky opened up revealing the magnificent view of heaven's past, present and future, time seemingly began to speed up its search for adulthood.

Prom came and went without the slightest notion of being important, with the ever closing-in effect of time pushing Sam and me toward a more drastic look at the possibilities that lay out in front of us.

Alan and I became more distant. His plans were materializing into reality, especially after his acceptance into The University of Maryland.

"Damn, man, you're in there," I said to him, excited after hearing the news.

"Yeah, Tony, I am for real about this man, just as real about this as you are about Sam. Good luck with that. I know you know what you're doing," he said, patting me on the shoulder as we stood in the very same hallway where our game had begun, "and take care of yourself in that military, too, Mr. Tough-Guy."

I actually felt the opportunity we created as friends slip away. He and I were walking down separate paths, after having carved them from the same general sense of purpose, love and being.

He was being true to his wants, and I felt I was being true to my needs. We were both growing and our words revealed the essence behind becoming a man.

Thoughts of a tattered past came rushing in, a past of me wanting to be noticed, wanting to be heard, wanting to be seen, just plain wanted. Not soon after that thought and vision

had left my head, I immediately pictured Sam
walking by, smiling graciously as she walked
through the hallway reading our dream come true
book. I knew I had not only made the right
decision of wanting to be Sam's man, but I had
also inadvertently cured the wound in my heart.

"Yeah bro', I know it, too," I said transformed by my new found reality of acceptance. I
felt I was taking care of me, for myself, without the need of an overseer. I no longer needed
to wonder what the hell I was doing here on the
Earth…Sam had literally walked into my world,
the exact opposite of my mother, representing
the lighter side of a woman I had always wanted
to love, giving me my reason for being.

The day before graduation, with little to
no money in my pocket, Sam and I went to our
favorite wooded park and took a walk. We had
gone a fair distance when I asked her to have a
seat on a tree stump of an old Oak that had
been cut down. The view overlooked the entrance
into a residential neighborhood with two-car
garages and manicured yards, all trimmed and
fenced in.

"Sam, I want that," I said, after she had
been sitting awhile looking up at me with concern as I looked out into the sprawling neighborhood in silence.

"You want what, Tony?" she asked, unsure of
what message I was trying to convey.

"I want that," I said again, pointing this
time toward the neighborhood, "I want a family.
It's something I've never had."

She said nothing.

"Sam, will you marry me?" I asked, unaware of the words that had fallen from my mouth until I heard her say...

"Yes."

We sat and held each other for what seemed like forever, taking in the passing moment.

We knew we had made a bond, a commitment, and a connection we both wanted but couldn't imagine how to follow to completion. The answers seemed too complex and out of the reach of the simple sounds of our words. So we said nothing.

Sam went to college, and I went away to boot camp. Every day between letters from Sam seemed void of everything except time and space. Boot camp was a breeze with my focus and intent placed firmly in my love for Sam and my desire to see her laugh with delight at seeing me as her Marine. Although the intensity of each moment brought me closer and closer to my goal of mastering boot camp and being a top recruit, I couldn't stop thinking about our vow.

"Listen up, recruits," our Heavy, the hardest of our three Drill Instructors (DI's), said in his gruff voice one morning as we marched to training. "Today is the beginning of hand-to-hand combat training. We will be doing puggel-stick training, to simulate the techniques and tactics of using your rifle as a tool of destruction in hand-to-hand combat. Whoever is the first to draw blood from his enemy gets a ten-minute phone call home.

Uurrah!!" he bellowed, followed by a spirit-filled Uurrah! from the platoon.

I knew in my mind I would be the one making that phone call home. I had to. I needed to hear her voice, to know she too was being moved and guided by our love and vow.

We stood between each other in a circular ring surrounded by all the DI's from the platoons. I could smell his fear and I wanted to take full advantage of it.

"Ready!" the Master Instructor yelled. "Kill!"

I quickly stepped to the left and swung my stick in a right to left slashing motion, hitting my opponent right between the eyes. His head dropped, and I countered with an upward slashing motion striking him squarely on the chin, continuing the momentum of the swing to his nose causing it to gush open like a geyser.

My Heavy was elated, telling all the other recruits to use my methods as the way to become a Marine.

All I could think about was talking to Sam, my motivation and my love.

I knew I wanted to be a Marine. I knew I would become a Marine. I wanted even more to know I was still loved by Sam, and using what I knew was going to help me find that out as well…helping me to hear her voice, to place the sweet smell of her letters with the delicateness of her thoughts of me, to ease my own thoughts of her not wanting to be, strengthening my reasons for being.

I called and got no answer, no machine and no reply.

I wanted nothing more than to hear her voice fill with excitement, knowing I was on the other end saying hello. I wanted to hear the sound of her freedom and experience away at school. I wanted to hear her say she loved me.

I took another recruit's night watch and gave him my phone time.

I couldn't sleep, I thought, so I might as well watch over my Marines.

Here I was in Marine Corps boot camp, one of the most mentally and physically challenging places in the world, and my thoughts and actions were being driven by love, I said to myself as I walked up and down the rows between the bunks pursuant to the rules of night watch. I must have been crazy.

Weeks later I received a letter from Sam, still laced with its beautiful scent, informing me she would not be able to make my graduation ceremony because of school. Once again disappointment filled me. I was graduating as one of the top recruits, embraced by the corps, but it had all been fueled by a passion to be Sam's badass Marine. And she wasn't going to make it.

At least the Corps loved me. I felt myself embrace those words as if they were the only things I had remaining from my escapade as a man.

Did I choose the wrong direction? I thought, letting the first concrete element of doubt concerning my ladylove slip in. I was determined to play it to the end.

On the eve of Graduation Day, families were invited to come and hang out with the recruits, visiting where we lived for the past three months, stump along our training grounds, and mingle with some of the other recruits from the various platoons. I planned to distance myself as far from the fiasco as I could, becoming more and more bitter at the thought of not having anyone there for me.

As we marched toward the designated area to meet our family members, I looked up and thought I saw a girl who looked like Sam. I quickly dismissed it as my mind playing tricks on me. Our formation broke and I walked alone toward the visitor center, drowning myself in the misery of love, when I heard someone behind me call my name. I turned around, and, for the first time since what seemed like forever, I felt tears falling down from my eyes. There before me stood my angel…the one I had dreamed of all my life.

She ran toward me and we embraced each other, and I could smell the lovely shade of strawberries and mango from her hair, meshed with a hint of vanilla adorning her bosom. I knew I was in heaven, and I didn't want to ever leave.

"Hey, Sam, can you believe it? We're actually moving into our own place. Isn't it exciting?"

She didn't answer right away, so I took my eyes off of the road and looked over at her. She had tears in her eyes.

"I'm scared, Tony. I love you but I am scared."

I slowly pulled over to the side of the road, put my hazard lights on, gently caressed her face and smiled.

I told her that it was going to be okay and that today was the beginning to the rest of our lives together as one.

"We have taken the first step toward building our own world together; it's a good thing, Luv," I said.

I was totally certain that this woman and I would begin a life that would become representative of a change in love and living, with so many hopes, dreams and aspirations wrapped in motivation. We had bid our time apart from one another; finding out love meant everything, wanting to be with one another, defying the logic of her parents and the wisdom of their experience. Her father told us no, we were not ready to marry and that he would not have me carry his daughter away like some long sought after prize. I stood tall in defiance, determined to prove I was more than worthy of her hand in marriage, flamboyantly announcing that it was out of honor and respect for him I asked for his daughter's hand, I was not seeking his approval to love his daughter for life. He stood fast. We eloped.

How could this be wrong? I thought, awakening from my rumbling through the boldness of our actions.

Besides, she was the love of my life, and I had known it from the first time I ever laid eyes on her. Seeing her now in this state of fear was comforting and exciting in some regards.

She counted on me to love her for life and wanted to take this leap with me, standing tall against her father's wishes, severing herself from the clasp of his deadly grip. I felt like I was the luckiest man alive.

"I know," she said. "We can do this."

So we continued on, headed toward our humble abode in Jacksonville, North Carolina, a nice little two bedroom flat, away from the town, but not too far in the country; it felt as though we really had it made.

She loved it and immediately started making plans to fill the place with her touch of home. I sat back and watched this innocent, young, creative, beautiful woman begin the cycle of coming into her own, and I was thrilled to be the one for her.

Life was beginning for me, with my two loves hand in hand. I had the Corps and I had my ladylove. What could be better?

This was easy; I was ready and so was she, and no matter the challenge, we were up for it, for better or worse.

Then came the moment of truth, our first major blow-up over nothingness.

"Tony, we need to plan a trip back home to see everybody."

"Baby girl, you know I can't do anything right now; I'm on air alert, and besides, our pockets are a little thin," I responded, feeling that I was defending a known thing -- the Marine Corps' rules for staying put in case of a need for rapid deployment, requiring us to leave at the spur of the moment by air, land or sea.

Now this one exchange into the conversation is where the apple cart began to tip.

It's funny looking back how balance became the most significant thing in my relationship between wife and Corps, but quite frankly the easiest thing to lose as well.

"You know, Tony, I'm growing a little tired of not having and putting my life on hold," she said, throwing her head back for good measure. "All I do is go to school and come home thinking today you and I will do this or that, then you call and say you're gonna be late or you have to do something with one of your Marines. What about me, Tony, don't I matter anymore?" she screamed, while storming down the hall with the fierceness of a North Carolina hurricane.

One love was attacking the other. I need to solve this now, but how? I thought, scrambling within myself for anything to make things right.

And which one was attacking whom?

And why?

Woooooooooooooo...I felt my mind say to my heart, as they entered into debate.

"Damn it, Sam, I am doing the best I can," I fired back with passion I hadn't felt since I outfoxed my man Alan to win Sam. "You know I love you; I said I care; I am here as much as I can be," I said, softening my words to a whisper while walking around to the side of the bed where she sat with tears rolling down her face. "You know I have to do the things I do because those are the responsibilities I took on with the Corps. But you know there's no comparison, right?" I asked, gently pushing her chin up. "Look at me, Sam, I love you."

This should do it; I felt my heart and mind agree with one another, easing the tension I had begun to feel, allowing me to connect with Sam in her state of disarray.

Band-Aid, a temporary fixer-upper and nothing more...

Action speaks louder than words, and my actions were focused in and on being a Marine who was married, although in love, according to Sam.

Being from the South and raised around women, I knew how to throw my whole self into trying to fulfill my love's dreams. So I stepped it up a bit.

"Hi Shortcake," I chirped into the phone one morning, crouched in a corner away from the others at work. I called Sam this on occasion teasingly because she stood five feet two inches, ten inches shorter than me, but much sweeter in my mind. "What time are you getting home from school tonight?" I asked.

Sam had decided, after spending a couple of years at a small private school in Colorado, we should be together. After I finished my mili-

tary job training courses, we were married,
albeit forcefully over the objections of her
father, and had settled in a bit, when she
decided to continue pursuing her degree in Pre-
Med.

"I don't know, washing my hair right now,
will be leaving here at about 12 or so, have
two classes and a study session, thinking maybe
of catching up with my classmate, Rita, afterward, so let's say around 8 or 8:30."

I had planned in my head to cook dinner and
have her a nice hot bath and a glass of wine
waiting when she got home. So, I needed to know
what time she was getting home. But I had to
say to myself, women take the long way to ans-
werville. Which prompted the question, "Are you
listening to me?" from her.

"Of course I am, Sam. I called to talk to
you remember. I am going to at least listen," I
responded smartly. "But, that's cool, I didn't
really want anything, just wanted to see how
you're doing. But I can tell you're edgy and I
need to get back to work anyway," I said, knowing I would agitate her to no end.

"Fine," she said, "see you later tonight,
love you, bye." She hung up abruptly.

Hook, line and sinker. I had her suffi-
ciently upset. When she got home, she would
not be expecting a thing.

I rushed home after work, ripping off my
cammie top and tee as soon as I hit the door. I
threw it toward the living room sofa and headed
straight for the kitchen.

Denver. I had totally forgotten about him
until I walked in the kitchen. He had shredded
all the paper towels and somehow managed to get
into the refrigerator. Food was everywhere.
From the ceiling to the edge of the entrance
into the dining room, food had found its mark,
with no dog in sight.

"Denver!" I yelled, feeling myself starting to flex, as my jaws and hands tightened. I was pissed. Not because of the mess as much as knowing I didn't have much time to clean and cook and find our dog, a Lab-Shepard mix bought as a house-warming gift and companion for Sam when I was away, now turned fugitive from my wrath and spoiler of my plans.

I corralled him out of his usual hiding spot under the bed and put him outside. I just couldn't believe he got in the refrigerator. Immediately I began scrubbing the kitchen as if I was in a fastest clean-up challenge, deter-mined to get it done before Sam came home. I had an hour and a half from the time she told me she was leaving, I thought to myself. I know I can do this.

I didn't.

Before I knew it, I saw the headlights of Sam's Camry pulling into the parking space in front of our house, and I had only gotten the kitchen floor mopped. Bags of trash were piled along the walls beside the laundry closet.

She walked in looking tired and disgruntled from the forty-five minute drive home and cer-tainly in no mood to deal with anything beyond a quick bite to eat, a bath, then climbing into bed.

"Hi babe how was class?" I asked, trying to break the forming iceberg brought in with her mood.

"What is going on here, Tony? And where is Denver?"

"He's outside getting some air. We had a little accident here I had to clean up, don't worry about it, just sit and relax a bit. I'll be done here in a second," I said, speeding up the swinging of my mop as I backed out of the kitchen into the dining room.

"You're always making a mess, Tony," she said as she walked down the hall into our bed-room.

I know I am, I thought to myself, but I will get it right.

"I ordered Chinese food, ShortCake, so you don't have to cook; we can just chill and talk," I said, following her into the room after finishing my unplanned chore. "And I got you a nice warm bath ready, too, and I'm bathing you," I continued, letting my eyes travel up and down her body.

I gave her a nice long hug from behind and began massaging her neck and shoulders.

"I just want to be with you, you know, show a little TLC. I know I've been busy lately and so involved with work and all, but you're still my number one love. You know that, right?" I whispered to her while nibbling on her ear.

"I know, Tony, I know, but sometimes I want you around more. I wanna know you care, that's all."

"I do. I do," I said as I kissed the nape of her neck, smelling the luscious smell of strawberries in her hair. "You're it," I said, pushing her on the bed, "and I am in."

"Well, come and get me then," she said with a devious smile while looking up at me with her dark brown baby doll eyes…

And what a sucker I was for those eyes…

Thirteen months had passed and so had the bliss of marriage, both to the Corps and to my new wife.

Sam, being a full-time student, was travel-ing back and forth forty-five minutes one way to school every day, and I, being a newbie in an infantry battalion, was gung-ho about making myself stand out as one of the best Marines in the battalion, creating a bad combination for the newness of our young love.

Next thing I knew, I was being told my commitment level was to the wrong love…again.

"Sam, you know I love you dearly; I am just not getting the point of what you want from me," I said, almost in tears, but, being a Marine, there was no crying on any job. "You know I am committed to you and want you, but I don't know how to make it much clearer that here is where I want to be," I said too many times to remember.

But too many more times, I heard her say –

"You need to show me more. I need you to be more receptive to my needs. I need you to listen to me, touch me, hold me, take walks with me, do nothing with me, something!"

From day one it seemed I was never around long enough to establish a significant, lasting connection with my new bride, spending nine months at sea, three months in Cuba, one month in Bridgeport, two months in 29 Palms, going and going and going.

Long nights and dragging days were spent trying to live up to the reality of being a man, a Marine, a husband, and a friend. Playing these roles seemed both impossible and improvable but beneficial and meaningful for all involved. I began to break down, feeling as though I was failing miserably, hoping for a sense of reprieve, a breath of freshness in love.

What a life, I thought, as I wandered around looking for the answers, the glue, to keep the pieces of my life in love aligned, while all the time thinking how strange real love seemed, with the incomparable words of Al

Green ringing in my ears: "It makes you wanna do wrong, do right."

Love made me blind. It made me forget the point of why I even started seeking it in the first place.

My mistakes showered upon me reality, making me regret having made choices that were the cause of so much pain for both Sam and I. My love didn't seem like love at all, but I didn't and couldn't listen to my mistakes enough from being blind.

I fought to establish her as the apple of my eye, knowing her father waited in the wings.

But, blindness remained clinging to the picture of uncertainty being made clear after hearing Sam say she loved me, it made me think that just being with her was enough, crushing my mistakes underneath my feet, rising me up to believe I had arrived soundly in the right place with love.

I still remember my 20th birthday, the end of our first year of marriage, like yesterday.

Sam managed to get all of my friends together to throw me a tremendous surprise party. All of my Marines were in on it, from my Gunny all the way down to the Privates who worked for me, and it was amazing to me that no one revealed what was going on.

My buddy, Aaron, was the main culprit.

"Hey, TL, let's go down a few after work, man," he said.

"No way, I better not; dude, you know how the lady can get about me not spending quality time with her, " I replied.

Out of my close knit group, which included Raul, the smooth brother from the Bronx; Keith, the laid back Kat from Buffalo; Juan, the excitable one from Cincinnati; David, the suave, analytical brother from Columbia; Jason, the Cowboy from Tulsa; and Dwayne, the leader from Hampton, Aaron, from the heart of Florida, was the feisty one and over the top convincing.

"Man, you know damn well if you're with me, she's gonna be cool about it," he said while pushing me out of the office toward the car. "Besides, who's the man anyway?" he asked, laughing loudly.

So, I went, eager to go tie on a few, oblivious to the set-up that awaited me. Being older, Aaron ordered the drinks and we sat and had one or two, embracing Captain and Coke as a friend, while enjoying a live bluegrass performance by a local band called Enuff, which was decent. The bar itself made the place, nice mixed crowd for a military town, lovely wait and bar staff, and circular wooden stage with the sitting and dancing area surrounding it… fittingly named, "The Stage."

"Let's blow this joint," Aaron suddenly said after 45 minutes or so, interrupting my vibing with the place and the music.

"Already? We just got here," I replied, a bit annoyed at being interrupted.

"Yeah, but like you said earlier, you definitely don't want your ShortCake to be stale, so let's roll," he said with a chuckle.

"True that," I said, finishing up my beer before leaving.

We got back to my house and Aaron mentioned that he had to use the bathroom. I thought he had to be an idiot for not using it before we left the bar, shaking my head as we walked toward the house.

He gave me the finger while I fumbled with my keys trying to unlock the door.

"Surprise! Happy Birthday to you," everyone began singing, as Aaron and I stumbled through the door.

I damn near fell back out of the door at the sight and sound of everyone yelling. I was immediately overtaken with a feeling of warmth, love and joy.

"Wow. Aaron you're a mutha-fucker, gotta watch you," I said, smiling and giving him a punch in the chest. "Damn, I never would have guessed this," I said to everyone, looking around at the decorations covering the living room, dining room and kitchen, not to mention the people jammed in our little two bedroom place.

"Thank you, thank you. I don't know what to say. Where's that wife of mine?" I asked, looking around.

I grabbed her in my arms and gave her a huge kiss to the sheer joy, handclaps and cat-calls from my boys and their significant others.

"Get her Devil-Dog," they yelled. "Uurrgh, Uurrgh," they grunted in typical Marine battle-cry fashion, with the ladies chiming right along.

It was awesome.

I appreciated her more than I could have ever imagined. I thought of her as my angel of joy. Up until then, I couldn't remember the last time someone had cared to celebrate my existence in such a grand fashion. Sam and I had always just been together on our birthdays. She made this one different for me, bringing me family in celebration of me.

I hugged everyone, expressing how much I appreciated them, my men and their loves.

It happened to be one of the best days of my life, and what better woman to help share it with me than the one I would readily die for again and again, I thought.

As a young man, with responsibilities that were sometimes not so easily understood, it was hard to grasp the severity of my situation.

But I tried...

The Marine Corps Ball of that year had me thinking for sure this would be an excellent time to make amends to my wife for my shortcomings as a husband, friend and lover and to unite her with the traditions of being a Marine. Newly charged with desire from Sam's tenderness, I was determined to become a Marine with a wife first before anything.

The ball was excellent, and my wife was the most beautiful woman, dressed in her blue evening gown, her hair pined up and curled tightly, revealing golden earrings dangling from her lobes like dusters, complementing the medals pinned to my dress-blues, palpitating my heart.

"Cinderella, may I have this dance?" I asked her after dinner and the ceremonial cake cutting. "You're beautiful," I whispered in her ear as I took her hand, leading her out on the floor.

After dancing as if we were the only ones around, we left early and went for a drive along the coast, listening to the waves crash against the sandy beach dunes. We pulled into a dimly lit area with a half-crescent moon beaming brilliant rays of light down on us.

It was magical.

Silence filled and grasped at the empty, void spaces of our hearts and minds, and for a moment we saw why we were we. We walked the coast-line, making plans and vows to keep our

love strong, thoughts of the future dangling
before us, shimmering off of my heart into
Sam's ears, looping us in our commitment to
love for life.

"Sam, remember when I proposed to you that
day…"

"Yes, like yesterday," she said, curling
herself closer to me, with my dress-blues coat
draped around her. "Why do you ask?"

"Well, I was thinking maybe we should consider starting a family. I would love to see a
little you running around. Wouldn't you?" I
asked, bracing myself for her reply.

"Tony, I want nothing more, except I think
maybe we should talk about it more. It's a big
step with no turning back, don't you think?"
she said, always the practical one of us two.

"Yeah, you're right. It sure would be nice
though," I answered.

"I love you, Tony. I'm not going anywhere,
and we will have our family in due time," she
said as the cold water washed over our feet.

"I know."

We drove away from the beach that night
thinking we had found a new stroke of love that
could carry us through for all times. The certainty within our minds and the beating of our
hearts seemed to ensure us we were meant to be,
forever and a day.

But the evening proved to not be magical
enough to emancipate us from the depths of our
fallen state of love.

It actually seemed to worsen it.

It seemed I just couldn't get the roles
right. I would always mix them up.

Go to work and be cordial and understanding
to my Marines, come home yelling and angry with
my wife…just mixed the hell up.

Six months after the night of our enligh-
tenment leading us to think we could and would
be okay, I received orders to be shipped to
Okinawa, Japan. Going overseas, in the condi-
tion that my marriage was in, began the beginning of a falling state for us, revealing the
extreme sense of no return for our love on the
rocks.

So, I talked with my Gunny, a serious position in the Corps, sort of next to god, and he
told me –

"Brown, if the Corps wanted you to have a
wife, it would have issued you one."

"But Gunny," I said feeling the pressure of
losing take grip, "this is my wife, for better
or worse, man, how am I supposed to keep things
going right here if my personal life is in
shambles?"

"Brown, you have to figure that out between
the two of you. Your life here in the Corps,
for all standard purposes, is apart from your
personal life. Just keep it together," he said.

Basically, let the chips fall as they may,
in the end you will get through it, either with
her or without her.

That's when I found out which love was more
demanding.

But I wanted Sam to be the top love; I
didn't think the right love had won for a long
time, going through the motions while at work.
I learned rather quickly that all the happiness
Sam and I once conjured up together no longer
blew through our sail of marital bliss.

During the time of rapid deployments, here, there and everywhere, I developed a strong personal relationship with a fellow Marine I met on a bus ride to our eventual duty station. He also had a wife he was leaving behind while we romped and stumped our way every-which-way but loose. And even more of a strike of coincidence, he had actually attended my birthday bash, courtesy of my wife inviting his. Raul was the smooth brother from the Bronx. In fact so smooth, I had hardly taken notice of his inverted mirror reflection of my problems.

"Brother, you have to relax and just love that woman of yours as if she was the last blade of grass in the city. Make her feel special, even when you don't know how, junior. That, my man, is what love's all about," he said to me as we flew over the Pacific, obviously after reading the look of despair all over my face.

"Yeah, but she didn't even shed a tear. It was as if I was saying good-bye to her forever," I said, starting to choke up at the mere thought.

"Relax and love, brother, relax and love," he said, closing his eyes as if he was going to Relax-And-Love-Land.

I thought to myself, that brother may be smooth as silk, but I feel like shrinking cotton. I no longer fit with Sam's desires.

I closed my eyes and began to run like hell.

Pretty soon after touching down and getting settled in Okinawa the bottle became my friend, specifically the Crown bottle… gotta have expensive taste, even in the midst of devastation.

My knees had taken a beating from a training regime in Cuba and deteriorated further during the first few months in Japan. I now needed surgery to repair my left one, which seemed ready to fall apart.

On top of that, I received what I already knew to be the truth, Sam's confession of our dying love, less than two months after being apart.

It was like receiving a slap to the face from the gates of hell.

There I was, a leader of Marines, comforting the young in mind about their girlfriends, and my wife was sending me a Dear John letter, expressing dissatisfaction on every turn of our time together.

"Dear Tony," she started, as if there was going to be anything dear about the rest of the letter, I thought.

"Things just aren't the same anymore…I love you but I can't…"

I stopped. I just couldn't get through the rest of the letter without feeling like I had lost it all…again…

"Baby, it's okay," my grandmother kept saying to me, over and over again. "She will always be here with you, I promise," she said, placing one hand over her heart and the other on her forehead.

My grandmother sat underneath my favorite pecan tree, trying to talk me down. She didn't understand that I didn't want to come down. In fact, I was never coming down. I didn't get how my mother could be gone when she was never around, and when she started to come around and try, like that she was gone. I didn't get it. So much for love conquers all, I thought, as I sat up in my tree, wishing I was far, far away...

On The Road…

Intertwined, interlaced, intermingled, interfaced
Let everything that has life breath the same
Lay claim to something, anything, and watch it all
change
Lessons reveal plenty - pure as driven snow
Causing chemical reactions to occur…
Blur against the face certain to reveal
Scornful it seems, until the scorn soon heal
Or perhaps someone you knew is scorned by you
Upsetting the delicate balance we all seem to share
The grip of a nation, a lover's stare
Being broken by a culling desire
Oh how we all aspire
To be free as sparrows, restful like dew…
In love with each other; in love with you…
Nonetheless watching the clouds zoom by
Leaves my heart bleeding blue…
Misfiring data, words of pain
B R E A K
      D

          O

            W
            N.   .   .

                        INSANE!

TL

still continued to exist.

I tried to call her, knowing she was many hours behind me in Japan. I just wanted to hear her say hello. But, she didn't answer.

I called her again and again and again, until she finally picked up, answering in a voice that seemed as if she had floated away.

"Hello," she whispered.

"Hi, I just needed to hear your voice," I said, fumbling through my words for the right things to say.

"Tony, you shouldn't have, we aren't meant to…"

"Don't say it, don't say it," I moaned. "I need you, Luv…I need you." I started to feel the tears build-up in the wells of my eyes. "I can't live without you ShortCake, it's all about you, always has been, always will be," I continued to moan, flushed with wetness running down my face.

"Tony, I can't," she said. "We're different. Besides, you wouldn't like me anyway. I'm not your me anymore. I'm not your girl," she said.

"What do you mean, Sam? I will always love you   no   matter…"
"NO!" she screamed, "I can't!" she slammed the phone down.

I sat and listened to the dial-tone singing a deafening sound of loss in my ear. I began to cry harder and felt like dying. My life was coming to an end, and there wasn't a DAMN thing I could do about it but die. Being damned was eternal.

I began drinking more.

It was as if I had nothing to prove, and nothing to gain or lose, so I drank, sat watching the time slowly trickle by, and plotted and schemed while working at my second job I picked up to help pass the time, washing dishes at a Japanese restaurant, thinking and organizing the many ways I would make it right when I got home.

It was going to be great, and I would start by turning back to The Rock!, God always looks out for the weak, I thought.

But before I made that stop at The Rock, I took the scenic route down the long highway into lost love…partying like I had damaged my last damn nerve.

When the music began to play and the party started, it was a Friday night, after a long exhausting week of work with my hands and rewinding with my head. I was determined to just get bent and let it ride.

Leaving work, I slowly jogged up the hill toward my barracks, taking my cammie top off as I went along, looking for any sign of activity from anyone I knew. I needed a drink to ease my aching pain. Sure enough, good ol'e Rob was sitting out in front of his room on the second floor, already dressed and having a beer, waiting for everyone to get back from work.

"Let's roll, man, you know we have to take the shuttle to Kadena and it's gonna take an hour, so we gotta catch this one," I said to my man, Rob. I had hurried through a shower, gotten dressed and packed up in 20 minutes after seeing him already in party mode, and was determined to waste no more time getting their myself.

Living on Camp Schwab, in Okinawa, was tough. Not only did we live far from everything going down in town, we had to take a bus to get there, too.

What a joke, I would find myself thinking during every bus ride.

Now Rob was a straight party freak. He could start at five, right after work, and go until five or six the next morning, and still would search for more to "kick-start" his morning.

Finally dressed, we dashed out the door, stepping it out to the bus stop.

We got to Kadena, and immediately after securing our passing out arrangements, went to a spot where the drinks just kept coming.

Before I knew it, I was dancing and feeling up on some mommie who must have thought I was worth the trip.

Club Inferno, what a spot, on a military base with military and local women, but enough sexiness oozing from them to make you want to pull up a chair. And there I was right in the middle of what some would call a little slice of heaven (and hell).

Freeze!

Yeah, that's me, sweat dripping in my drink, tongue hanging out my mouth and eyes wilding out, then I stumble and find myself wondering, "where am I?" out loud.

The girl I was dancing with looked at me and said, "Are you ok, you look a little freaked out or something?"

I said, "Thank you," and walked off the floor headed for the bar.

For what, I don't know.

So, I sat down at the corner of the bar, away from the glare of the dance floor and just observed.

I soon realized the girl and I were still on the floor dancing, but here I was sitting.

What the hell, I remember thinking. Then I sobered enough to know I was having some kind of experience...

I upchucked.

Lifting my head up from my great reprieve, I found myself back again, looking at the melting of bodies, lights, smoke and sound.

I walked.

The next day Rob was infuriated.

"What the hell happened to you last night? I looked around and you were gone."

We had rented a hotel for the night, and he found me there the next morning sitting on the bed, staring out the window into the bay.

"Man, I think I had a revelation last night, dude," I told him.

"I'll say, the way you explored that girl on the dance floor, I bet a lot was revealed to you," he said chuckling, while sipping a beer (good 'ole Rob).

I laughed his comments away, drifting out toward the calming waves cresting against the pier.

The next day while walking down the streets of Camp Schwab, still feeling the effects of my experience, I ran into Raul walking at a faster pace in the opposite direction, looking as if gold awaited him at the other end of the base.

"Hey what's up, T, where you headed?" he asked with a bright smile on his face.

"To die," I responded. The thoughts of my loss came rushing back in.

"What's going on with you?" Raul asked, stopping in front of me with an look of concern in his eyes. "Anything I can help you with, Tony?"

"Raul, I wish you could, but the fact of the matter is you can't, unless you have some kind of voodoo you can use on my unhappy wife.

She's leaving me man," I said, fighting back tears.

For awhile we just stood there, facing the East, watching the Sun come up over the gates of Camp Schwab, when finally Raul broke the eerie silence of the day break.

"Bro', come walk with me for a while," Raul said, turning back toward the beach.

"It's going to be alright, man. Sam just don't know what she wants right now and this may be an opportune time to find out who you are as well bro'," he said. "I mean, God works in mysterious ways, and for all you know, He may be preparing you for something."

"Raul, no offense man, but god is a mother-fucker. Why would a god allow this now?" I said.

"I don't know, but maybe you should ask Him," Raul said as we jumped across the rocks along the coastline of the beach along Camp Schwab.

"Maybe I will."

I started to go back to church, the prover-bial Rock, with Raul. Something there had to show me some guidance, give me some clue, allow me some kind of saving grace. I grew up bap-tized in the belief that when all and everyone else failed to love you, God still did. I stu-died The Word, feverishly as a kid, sheltering myself from the darkness with the words of prophecy. For a while even I was being groomed to preach the gospel according to Christ.

"Baby, God has put his anointing on you," my grandmother said. *"He wants you to carry his message to and fro', Tony, because he has found*

*favor in you and how you make His words cleanse
others' fears."*

*I didn't know about favor. I felt staying
alive amongst the violence of hateful men my
mother brought into our world surely couldn't
be a blessing, but I listened anyway and kept
on praying prayers that made people shout for
joy and scream Hallelujah! I just couldn't see
love anywhere else, so it had to be in words
that made people feel good.*

Church on the island, dressed in fatigues,
hugging and praying, studying and bonding, all
in the name of love, was a stretch for my imagination.

Is this real or just an effect of loneli-
ness? I found myself wondering one evening as
the prayers of the leader of our group went
throughout the chapel escaping out the windows
in the atmosphere all around us.

Wake-up! the light streaming back through
the windows seemed to scream, countering the
words of our prayer leader.

I did.

I walked.

Marines past and present say there are only
three things one can do while in Okinawa, especially those on the infamous Camp Schwab: lift
weights and become a fit freak, engross oneself
in the companionship of alcoholic beverages, or
baptize oneself in the world of being a holy
roller. Well, I did all three, and I was going
back to the States somehow juggling them.

Ready or not, Sam, here I come, buffed and
full of desire... And the rest is history... ancient history it seems sometimes, but not all
the time, like now...

Blue

What does it mean when you say her name?
Does it require pain or gain?
How does it feel?
Do you really know?
Maybe, it's just a show...
Stop and listen.
Feeling the vibe?
Open up and let it flow.
Is there anything to hide?
What is it anyway that makes the world go 'round?
Is it really force or a joyful sound?
Life is full of questions, isn't it so?
Until one day you let it flow; you know?
All things come to pass.
Isn't that true?
Look up to see through...
The world is blue –
Because of you...

TL

She was ready.

I got back to the States, excited and still hopeful, looking out the window to see if there was a banner for me among all the other banners greeting the Marines as we rolled back into town. I searched with my eyes and my heart, looking and hoping for one for me with my name on it reading, "Welcome Home, Tony! I Love You – Sam."

But, of course, there was no banner.

What was waiting for me was a note from Sam, with the keys to my black '93 Nissan Sentra, nicely detailed and trimmed out in gold.

I tore open the letter, still a little bit hopefully, thinking maybe this was one of her creative ways of making me want her more…she was so good at that, I thought. I opened the letter.

"As you can see I have left you, like I said I would…"

I hadn't read beyond the introduction to my "Dear John" Letter, so I didn't know she had planned on not being around when I returned.

And I shouldn't read this shit either, I thought, stopping myself enough to plan a counter attack, getting through the opening words.

"I should have known," I said aloud in a murmur, feeling my stomach drop as if a piece of my heart had fallen from my chest, forever lost.

The note continued with the revelation that my wonderful wife had packed up the house, since I had orders to Quantico, Virginia, and moved ahead of me, dropping our things in a storage unit until we could sort out the ownership of items in a divorce proceeding.

My heart screamed.

Okay, okay, I can handle this, I thought, and I fast-forwarded the next few weeks away in my mind, putting myself in position to win back the love of my wife once I arrived in Virginia.

I was high on Double O...Overly Optimistic.

After getting situated in one of the vacant, cellblock-shaped rooms in the barracks, I tried to contact Sam -- to no avail. My optimism slowly seeped away, and my mind turned toward deviant thoughts.

In the midst of my sorrow laced with anger, I started clubbing again with my Marine buddies, covering up my pain of a loss with loss of common sense.

Marines party hard and party long, so a few weeks was more like a few months, with very little sleep and very little sober time, but lots of woman chasing.

Check it out, I told myself as we prepared every evening for a long night on the town.

Just back from six months in Japan, I hadn't really heard all the latest craves, tight songs and new catch-lines to hook the big fish. We walked into Club Elsewhere with Busta Rhymes yelling at us through the loud speakers; telling us to jump, jump.

"T, you ready to do this man?" Rob asked me. "We haven't been home in a minute, and we got some catching up to do," he said while licking his lips and rubbing his palms together.

The next thing I knew he was bumping and grinding on the dance floor, devouring some fine Puerto Rican mommie dressed in a short mini without even waiting for my response.

I gathered myself and proceeded on my way, cutting through the crowd, headed straight for the bar, conveniently located on the backside of the dance floor. I was looking to wet my pallet with an old trusty and all-time favorite, Captain-n-Coke with a lime squeeze. To help me see and feel, I told myself.

One by two the ladies came streaming in, and I got full from one to the next.

I loved them all.

Women, what beautiful works of art! Such an imaginative creator we have…nice full hips with suckable lips, sweet smell and nice round tails…flowing like honey, shining like dew…what wonderful forms of life, my mind kept teasing me.

During this parting rendezvous of my mind, where I found myself letting my eyes pleasure my thoughts, I met a young woman who stopped my thoughts dead in their tracks, setting my eyes on her graceful form, Sweet Belinda.

It has been said the best way to get over one woman is through another. While I had always taken this as being cynical and cold, it began to ring with truth and devastation as the captain began to take over, loosening my thoughts, massaging my tongue.

"Damn," I said when I first saw her, knowing my hunt was over. I had found what I wanted and was going in for the kill.

She stood there with her baby brown doe eyes, curly hair, sexy full lips, cocoa buttery skin, shapely hips, 36/38 c-cups, tight stomach, long trimmed legs and pulling-appeal, dressed in a black cat-suit, calling for me, daring me to come over, as she stood there rocking next to her girlfriend, the protector of her innocence.

I floated over to her, my green and brown-checkered vest on and open, revealing my pecks

and abs, all the while flexing my biceps I
worked so hard on while in my funk of depression at Camp Schwab.

I began rubbing my shaved head, running my
hand down across my mustache, as I slowly approached.

No drink buying, I thought as I approached
thinking of one of my rules of thumb, never buy
a drink; once you do, it's like trying to close
a sale. For me, it's about opening a venture,
something to explore short, medium or long
term, with the possibilities of a sale to occur
at a later date.

"What's up, sexy, how you feeling?" I asked
as I moved in on her, stirring my drink in
hand, continuously flexing. " I felt you calling me from across the room, so I had to see
what you wanted and to assure you I got what
you need," I crooned to her, knowing I looked
good, sculpted to a solid 205 pounds of pure
man.

"Hi," she said, flashing a smile that almost made me begin to mumble mantras and shout
out parables, "I'm fine and, yea, I called you.
I wanted to see if you could work it as good as
you looked," she said.

"Would you like to find out?" I asked,
wasting no time.

I wanted to pull her close to me as soon as
I could. I wanted to feel her, smell her and
even taste her.

She accepted.

I placed my drink on a ledge that ran along
the wall and we rocked to LSG's groove "My Body
All Over Your Body" piping through the club. I
tried my best to determine what kind of perfume
she was wearing.

"Boy, you sure are working it," she whispered while trying to remain modest and stern.

But she couldn't help it.

The night belonged to us.

We danced and danced, getting caught up as if in an enchanted world of make-believe-come-true.

"Can I buy you a drink?"

"Sure, baby, why not," she said, "why not."

So much for rules.

Just like that, I broke the one that made me stay cool and in control. But there was something about this woman I needed to know, and I was willing to find out what it was by any means necessary.

She was a woman of control and grace, and was able to look at me for who I was, right then and there, what I was becoming, and somehow see what I needed to avoid. She expressed this with tenderness and sincerity. On the spot. It was amazing.

She knew, as if she were reading it all over my face.

"What are you doing here?" she asked me, after taking a sip of her strawberry daiquiri. "You look as if you lost something and hope to find it again," she said.

"No, it's not like that. I just got back from Japan and I miss this. So, I decided to let it all hang loose," I responded as coolly as I could, with laughter.

"Ummm hmmm," she said, not buying it. She smirked at me with such a draw; all I could do was lean over and kiss her.

It felt as though I was kissing a goddess. She had been cut from the cloth of passion, desire, lust, love, and sweetness, all wrapped in a fiery shell. And I didn't want to walk away from her. She was heaven sent, or, for all I knew, straight from the gates of hell, with sweet temptation. Not too pushy, not too standoffish, not too brash and not too soft, she

embodied what I needed at the moment...an escape from expectations.

What a view.

As the night came to an end and the bar
staff began kicking us out into the nighttime
breeze of Carolina air, I finally caught up
with Rob again.

"Hey bro' you wanna go grab something to
eat?" he asked, with the Rican-cutie in the
black mini hanging over his neck, nuzzled in
close. "Who's that sweet thing over there?" he
asked. "Bring her with, man," he said, bouncing
toward the car, not waiting for me to say either yes or no.

I turned toward Belinda, realizing she was
hanging out behind me with her girlfriend
standing point.

"Hey, Sweets, did you want to go grab something to eat?" I asked

"Sure, "if you ride with us."

"Belinda, we have to go," her over-
protective girlfriend said rather strongly.

"Hi, I'm sorry, I haven't had the pleasure
of meeting you, yet," I said, interrupting her
attempt to spoil the moment.

"My name is Tony," I took her hand and
softly kissed it. "It's nice to meet you."

"I'm Rachel," she said blushing, "likewise."

"Well, Rachel, what do you say we all go
and grab a quick bite to eat and I promise to
let you two go without harm, well, maybe a bite
here or there, but no major damage," I said
laughingly, while walking with my arms around
the waist of both ladies, toward their red
Toyota Celica with a black rag-top.

"Besides, it will be fun, especially once you drop the top and let your hair down," I said, giving Belinda a kiss softly on her neck.

We all went to breakfast and talked about life, love and the pursuit of happiness and peace, in one way or another, with my boy Rob trying to work magic on both Rachel and his Rican friend.

Before we knew it, the time on the clock was screaming 5:15am, and we all knew we had to go our separate ways.

Belinda and I vowed to see each other again soon, with no scheduled time in the making.

We both had other people, things and situations to iron out on our own, without adding the complicated math equivalent of another to the mix.

Through my short interaction with Belinda, I found I knew very little in the game of love and needed a teacher of sort to not only show me the error of my ways, but also make me aware of where I stood. I needed to know who I was without the outlook of pleasing someone else first. I needed an awakening.

We met again on my final move from Carolina to Virginia. It had been two months since the last time I had seen her, a month since the last time I had spoken to her, but it seemed like yesterday since the last time I touched and smelled her. She magically took me away from thoughts of worry, my wife and the end of my life, as I had known it.

Wrong or right, "this feels good," I said to myself as I drove along a winding country road through North Carolina, thinking back on my grandmother's vision of God's purpose for me.

Did it involve me finding me for me, first? I thought.

That felt impossible, since everyone else seemed to matter so much more.

I called Belinda on the way up that lonely North Carolina highway, filling my head with some old Teddy Pendergrass' lyrics, and she took the time to see me, so we could share one last moment in time.

The hotel room was dark, smelly and cramped, but the anticipation of being in her company again made it seem as though I was waiting in a five-star luxury suite.

She walked through the door, and we both beamed with joy and complete want.

Wanting to be there, wanting to say so much, wanting to not let go, wanting to begin anew, wanting to do nothing, wanting to lay and hear each other's heartbeat, wanting to cry, wanting to laugh, wanting to die…wanting to fly.

"I feel alive and wanted again," she said, while I wiped tears from her eyes, "and I know I can't have you and you can't have me, but I'll always treasure these moments for the rest of my life. You're special," she whispered, with her head cradled in the indented spot between my shoulder and the left side of my chest, perfectly positioned, in line with the drum beating of my running heart.

I didn't know what to say.

I had never even heard my wife say those words before.

I never knew love could be so simple and so pure, but so wrong and so blue.

Belinda and I had over the course of a few short months developed a need and desire for each other, even while knowing the ride was going to come to an eventual dead-end.

"Belinda, I don't know what's happened here with us, but I do know I haven't felt this way about many things before. Shit, I know I feel something for you that would make me do just about anything for you. I…"

"Shhhh," she said.

We laid and listened to each other without words, letting the energy of desire take us over, mere sex being nowhere near our minds, caught in a modified state of tantric lovemaking, allowing ourselves to see each other in one another, entangled within our desire to be loved.

It was peace and love converging and I knew it.

She began the process of opening up my third eye to the world of dreams beyond limits in love. But I still didn't quite grasp the fleeting experience of absolute love, something Belinda herself hadn't consider in her own life either, which made it easier for her to gravitate toward me.

She was an angel in disguise for me, and I guess, I was in turn hers.

We parted ways for the final time, vowing to always love and keep each other in our hearts, minds and spirits.

It ended as quickly as it began, like a figment of my imagination. It left a thought that had manifested itself as a lesson for me to learn. It expanded a moment that would link me to a true essence of absolute. It was an awakening epiphany. It was my first dance with the mystical feeling of living life in love with love.

While continuing my drive through North
Carolina, I began to want nothing more than to
show Sam that I had started learning how to
love her the right way now.

I could still hear Belinda's words, "You
have to be careful who you love, how you love
and why you love. You can be so much for someone and they may not be receptive because of
the way you present it. Sometimes you can be
over-the-top and other times you are reserved,
not many women have had a man like you," she
said.

"Yeah but…"

"Think about it, then act," she said,
gracefully interrupting me.

*************Tipping Point************

You Know...

Fundamentally speaking, all things are the same,
Looking around, one gets confused, then starts the game
Noise trickles in like steady pouring rain
Slowly but surely beginning to shape your name
Stopping only ever so often to let you suck it in –
When... When... When... WIN!... my friend
Instantaneously one knows – Darkness all around
With just a little light seeping through from a
distant sound
STOP!
     Listen!
        Follow that flow...
That is, if one wants to grow...
As easy as it seems to not re-invent the wheel
'Tis true but only for zeal
Deep inside of every being continuous nature resides
Not a vortex or a venture well known as pride
But a vessel, a path, a current that always go...
Shhh!!
     Listen some more
        Now you know...
Bringing forth a thirst so strong – water cannot quench
A tingle so deep from within one dares not flinch
For it's easy now to see and this is for real
Being driven by the way in which all is healed
Isn't it funny how life always finds a way
Look, listen and feel the beat... life is here to stay...

TL

***********Tipping Point***********

WARNING: CURVY ROAD AHEAD, I read as I speed along Route 24.

I knew Sam had to have gone to live with a friend of hers Arlington Heights. I was there already in my mind, my body needed to catch up.

Knocking on Cynthia's door, Sam's best friend, I felt a power surge go through me that would have allowed me to knock down the damn thing if I kept pounding. So, I stopped. I placed my hands in my pockets and began to whistle, as if this was the great day of reclamation. My face was vibrant and my heart was gleaming when the door finally opened and I saw her standing there.

My strength immediately left me, and my passion turned to fear…fear of loss, fear of failure, fear of regret, fear of facing the demons, just plain fear of the unknown.

Her face told it all.

I was looking into a mirror of hopelessness and despair in love. I swam on, knowing at that precise moment of our reunion that it had ended; it was finished. It was dry.

"Hello, Sam. I came by to ask you to lunch with me," I said, sounding awkward, and a little confused.

"Sure, we can go to lunch," she said. "Come on in, I have to get ready."

I walked through the door, thinking I had just penetrated the walls of my lost Love's fortress.

This may be a good move after all, I thought.

We went out for a walk, lunch and a talk. No sooner had we stepped off the curb from her building than she turned to me and said, "I have no desire to work out the issues in our relationship. I have found I am a much different person than the one you married, and like I told you before, you would not like me at all, especially now with your new found beliefs."

I immediately began to beg.

I pleaded.

I transformed.

I acted. I shouted.

I screamed, to no prevail…

"Tony, a lot has changed since you left in December. I'm not your wife any longer; I feel free, unmoved by you and alive again, and I like it," she happily revealed.

The steam rose up my neck, slowly building up in my ears, eyes and head. I was about to blow.

"Sam, I know things weren't perfect between us, but you have to know the best is to come," I said, smiling widely. "We can have children and travel and enjoy each other. I promise. I have seen what it could be. Let's start over, please. I need you," I said, reaching out my hand toward her, feeling as though I was on my last bow.

This woman, my girl, my first, my heart, looked me in the eye and said –

"There is no more me and you; we are through, and for that I am sorry. That's the way it is."

I became more mindful of us being out in public, walking in and out of the shops, so I kept my cool.

But, I could feel myself becoming increasingly weighed down with the agony of defeat. I knew I wasn't the same, but I persisted on the wings of a dying Pegasus, knowing I had been

born from a lineage of lust, deceit and destruction, with beauty still residing in my
being and a need to be loved and to show love
in return. And being a Marine, a man on a mission, a fool in love, I was determined to win
out and face down the pain of no longer being
wanted. I felt reinforced by the words that
seemingly sprung forth from her lips with ease.
It was a devastating blow of pain to not only
my heart, but all the way down to my reason for
being!

It was time to make a change. Her words had
set me on fire.

She entered a make-your-own jewelry shop
and was busy putting together a necklace in the
back of the store. I slowly walked over toward
her and began helping.

"You may not want to do that," she said.

I smiled, having re-gathered myself.

"Do what?" I cooed.

"You may not want to help me make this
necklace because I am making it for my friend
and I know you don't want to do that," she said
without the least bit of hesitation.

Ballgame! All the alarms in my body seemed
to chime at once, trying to avert my hell-bent
desires to sacrifice myself, with the words of
Keith Sweat "How Deep Is Your Love" swimming
throughout my head, oozing out of my ears.

At that moment, I knew the wind had been
completely let out of our sail, leaving me
stranded in a sea of misery.

I looked at her and she continued on, like
nothing else even mattered.

"So it's like that, huh? I go away, come
back and you haven't just moved on, but with
another? Why? How? When?" I asked, with a
throbbing feeling of explosion. "Shit, who's
the mutha-fucker?" You know, it doesn't even
matter, but god damn!" I said with a forceful

whisper. "I really loved you and I wanted us, and you are willing to flush it all away!" I said, slamming the beads down.

I didn't give her a chance to respond. I turned and walked away, storming out of the store into a rain-developing afternoon, a great compliment to my new state of being.

I walked toward an open air park a few blocks away from the shop and made my way toward the swings, sitting in one with my head hung low, asking myself, through my thoughts, through my blood, through my spirit, why? As though the answers would magically appear...

"I'm sorry, Tony, I never meant to hurt you," I heard Sam's voice coming from above me. "He's just a friend."

I looked up and realized she had followed me to the park.

I shook my head and said nothing.

"People change, things happen and we have to go with the flow, no matter how life altering it can be. We can't be afraid to trek into the unknown," she said, as if she was trying to not only teach me but to reassure herself as well.

Again, I said nothing.

"Goodbye, Tony, I will always love you, no matter what you think right now."

I looked up as she walked away and let the tears stream down my waterlogged face, knowing life as I knew it was melting away...and the rest is history, ancient history it seems sometimes, but not all the time, like now...

From Darkness

From darkness comes…
The morning dew
From nothingness are me and you
Yet, it is night that bring forth the fun
Pondering for another one.
It is through the emptiness of black
One can distinguish this from that
From darkness sparkles the light of day
Showing forth the beauty of next to NOne…
The Sun.
Springing forth from the depths of low, a creature is born
From darkness rose the breath of life in all
Oozing forth, it penetrates the thickest of the thick
Saturating all it sees.
Darkness shows the emptiness of space
From darkness we have the human race
From darkness comes…

TL

Saki, a favorite British author of mine, once wrote, "Romance at short notice was her specialty," and the same could be said of my lost love. I quickly came to realize, during my moment of loss that religion was only a theory getting me through adversity and turmoil. I also found that if and when the heat turned up in my life, my mind scrambled, and the results of my actions toward Sam and others I sought relationships and love from were sacrilegiously accomplished. Marvin Gaye's tune "Mercy, Mercy Me" played over and over again throughout my being, solidifying my mood, justifying my delirium.

Love had a tendency to take more than it had given in my life, so I hypnotically convinced myself into believing that going forward, I would become the Taker. I was living in, as the Hopi would say, Koyaanisqatsi, completely out of balance with love, without even knowing it. I was living through complete hell, a contorted mirror-like reflection exposing my dilapidated life.

I was in a time in which my whole existence changed, a time when my friends became more like family.

My man Bobby was a hip-hop fanatic who could pull together the best of the greatest lyricists, and make the music fit the scheme of our lives.

"Check this out, man," he said, putting one
of his CDs in as we sat in his car watching the
rain starting to fall.

We sat for a moment with Eric Sermon, Red-
man and Keith Murray "Don't Make No Sense"
breaking it down in the background for us, and
for a moment Bobby's words and mine seemed to
linger and mix, painting a picture of the love
lost to the beat of real hip-hop, making it all
okay.

"Bro, you know it is only a matter of time
before you're gonna be running the streets
pulling them in again. But this time, protect
your heart a little better," he said, while the
bass matched beats with the thundercloud passing overhead.

"I know you wanna be loved, but everybody
don't and can't be what you want, man. You a
big-dog, T, not many can run with you, bro.
Accept that shit and go have some fun until she
comes man. You hear me?" he asked, extending
his fist out to me.

"Now let's get inside this gym so I can
kick your ass."

I did hear my man, but I didn't feel him.

I couldn't meet him half way.

I just wanted to run and go play...

- -

Half-way through game three of a full-court
pickup b-ball battle we joined inside the gym,
I began to feel tight and knew I needed to stop
before I caused myself more pain than I was
willing to bear.

"Eh, B, I'm done, man. I need to go lift
for a while to get the strength in my legs
back," I yelled to Bobby as we came up the
floor.

I motioned for one of the many guys standing on the side to come and take my place,
blocking out Bobby giving me hell.

"You're getting old, boy," he said to the
delight of all the others on the court.

"Naw, just damaged," I chuckled as I jogged
off toward the weight room, proving I still had
gas in my tank.

As I walked around looking for a leg exten-
sion machine to use, the thought of having a
new lease on life came to me, and I began to
smile. Although I felt empty, I knew things
were going to be fine, having only my smile
left to show.

"Excuse me brother, I don't mean to bother
you," I heard a voice say from behind me. "But
I had to come over and let you know, man, that
your smile lights up the room. What's up with
you? Why so happy?" he asked, smiling with his
arms folded across his chest, waiting for my
reply.

My first impression was to guard myself.
But when I looked into his eyes, I saw no
threat of any kind, instead feeling a sense of
warmth, welcoming, sincerity and trust radiat-
ing from him, as if he was communicating with
me on some other level.

"Well, honestly, I am on the verge of divorce. I have a blown out left knee that's
threatening my Marine Corps career. My family
doesn't exist and I don't know why I'm here. I
have nothing left but to smile and wonder," I
said.

"Well, Tony, I gotta tell you, god has
great things in store for you. You ain't suppose to be married until you listen to love,
which will lead you to your purpose. He has
found favor in you, man. I am just telling you
what I see," he said before turning and walking
away. "Just keep smiling," he added as he

walked out of the gym without telling me his name, leaving me feeling like I was on Candid Camera or some weird prank show.

I shrugged it off and continued to work out until my legs felt rubbery, as though I had borrowed Stretch Armstrong's.

I told Bobby about my run-in with the stranger and asked if he had seen him leave or not. He said he had seen nothing and even suggested I was loosing it, making excuses for not being able to hang on the basketball court.

"What does love have to do with basketball, B?" I asked him jokingly, switching the subject.

"Everything, especially when you loose," he said, punching me in my ribs, getting me back from my earlier attack, then dashing toward the car parked across the street from the gym.

"Touché," I moaned, grimacing from the pain.

Needless to say, Sam and I started those divorce proceedings, ending the love affair of all love affairs. It's funny how life throws you curve balls when you're expecting fast ones.

Time began to drag on while I sorted the affairs of my heart, busy cataloging away the moments of my time with Sam, intensified by the looming date of our eventual end.

Do we make time what it is?

Do we establish the significance to the meaning of our moments?

Is our world shaped by what we take in and let out?

Is time irrelevant?

I found myself lost in a sea of questions, seemingly with little to no answers at all.

As the ever imaginative Joe would say, "Love don't make no sense"… And the rest is history…ancient history it seems sometimes, but not all the time, like now…

As Days Go By

What if you knew, how would it be,
If it was somehow revealed I was you and you were me,
Would things change or would they cease,
Could you handle it, would there be peace?
As time bleeds away, would it make you cry,
Would you do nothing or would you just fly,
I ask these simple questions, expecting a simple reply,
Knowing good and well where intentions lie…

What if you knew the secret to it all,
Would you tell your tale or ponder and stall,
Harder things may come, for power can restrain
Smart people from coming out of the rain,
Nightfall brings about all sorts of things,
May be best to just let it sting,
Truth shows we all know the way,
Reality is we all like to play…

I often sit and try to see,
Where all of this leads for me,
The moments occur, becoming oblivious
Life makes us all delirious,
Grasping, controlling, holding on,
Prolongs this slow, methodical dance song…
Let go, float away, walk in the clouds,
Stand up, shout it out and be damn proud…

TL

I'm good, I'm straight, I told myself one night as I stretched and squirmed across my bed looking out the window into a night, absent of star play.

"Right?" I found myself saying out loud to the walls, half-expecting to get a resounding reply.

I thought I had learned my lesson.

I thought I had grown up.

I thought I had gotten some wisdom, understanding and discernment concerning love and guidance, choices and decisions.

But, I wasn't counting the X-factor.

During the time when my lovely wife was making her decision, Cynthia was the friend helping her get through the difficult period of finding herself. As luck would have it, Sam decided some things were more important to her than others, even more than her friend who came to her rescue

So, the phone calls began.

"Tony, can we talk?" I heard a familiar and sexy voice proposition me from the other end of my car-phone, making me feel as though she was sitting next to me whispering sweet nothings into my ear, while I sped along I95-North on my way home from work.

"Who is this?" I asked, trying to match the freshly developing fantasy that was unwinding my day of hell into magical moments of ecstasy.

"Tony, you don't know my voice by now, as many times as I have called your house looking for your so-called wife…"

"Oh, hey, what's up girl?" I interjected, realizing it was Cynthia, maiming my vision of droplets of perfection from heaven.

"Nothing much, just thought it was about time I freed your ass from this shit you're dealing with."

"What? What's going on, Cynthia? You sound a little pissed or something. What did Sam do to you to get you this worked up? And by the way, I am free from it all. Our divorce is final," I said, making sure she knew Sam's and my boat had sunk.

"I'm just tired of supporting someone who isn't supportive of me and I damn sure was tired of watching you give chase when I knew you wasn't gonna ever catch her. Meet me at Bennigans in Alexandria; we can talk more there."

"Cool, I'll see you in 20," I said, pushing the accelerator down hard, now a bit anxious to hear this new developing, love closing straw of hope being torn to pieces before me. I had a right to know, I told myself, feeling a throb in my heart.

Cynthia and I met in the entranceway of Bennigans, embracing one another as if in mourning. We had a few beers at the bar and began talking away, both angered by our loss of someone so precious and dear to our hearts, both oblivious to the effects of the alcohol making us even more vulnerable.

"Let's go shoot some pool," I said, trying to break the depressive feel of our conversation.

"Tony, I am glad you got away from Sam. She was losing it, chasing some man in North Carolina while you were away. I feel bad for helping her out; I thought she wanted to start over," Cynthia said, unable to let go easily. "I didn't realize it was with another man, if I only knew…" she said, fading off into her thoughts. "I guess that's why we aren't tight anymore. She even chose him over me," Cynthia said while leaning across the table, stretching sexily along the length of her pool cue, licking her lips, trying to concentrate on her shot.

I sipped my beer and watched, finally breaking away from the loveliness of the image in front of me to ask –

"So, what happened between you two? I didn't realize it was like that. I never saw you not being friends."

"After she met with you that day at my place, she asked me to ride with her back to Jacksonville. I agreed. We split up when we got there and she had me hang with some of her guy friends by myself while she was with her man. That pissed me off, but I was cool about it. Then when we were leaving to come back here, she decided to ride with him and his buddy and leave me in the car alone. I was furious. Next thing I know," she said, getting visibly upset as she scratched one shot after the other, hitting the cue with force. "I sprang a flat and I didn't have anyone around to help me. Luckily some guys stopped and helped me out, but I was done with her after that weekend. I thought I was better off without her and you were definitely better off, and I hope you know that," she said to me, looking me straight in the eye, batting her eyelashes, pulling me into the strength of her resolve to be okay.

It was as if she had said the magic words, unleashing me from a spell or casting one, because I immediately felt released from the grasp of my loss. I had to connect the why, and

here Cynthia stood. She was leaning across the
red-fabric pool table positioned in front of me
looking like a Courvoisier commercial, and with
slow, delicate, precise brush strokes, began
painting a picture of brilliance for me, loosening me from my prison of pain.

"Yeah, you're right. I tried. I know I
wasn't perfect, but damn, I loved her and
wanted to be all the man I could for her. I
failed, but it's cool," I said with a strong
sense of confidence I hadn't felt in awhile.
"Life is a party with many rooms," I said with
a wink toward Cynthia.

"Your shot," she said, motioning the tip of
her cue toward me.

Both prone to trash talking, we decided to
place a wager on the game.

I had to break out my best skills.

But those legs and thighs kept getting in
my way, not to mention the way she presented
herself…sexy personified, woman enough to take
care of herself, but just enough of a lady, a
damsel without distress.

"Cynthia, you can't faze me girl, that's
your ass right there," I bragged as I pocketed
the eight ball to end the first game.

She looked at me and said -

"Beginner's luck. Besides, you haven't even
seen all my skills yet. So, how do you know you
got my ass?"

Damn, now it's on, I thought, and boy was I
ever so off base with my thinking, as Miles
Davis' tune "I Fall In Love Too Easily" satu-
rated the next seven minutes.

She won the second game by way of a scratch
on my part.

The third game we only got through pocket-
ing one ball.

During a trip around the table, we rubbed up against each other and the fire began to roar.

"What are you doing, Tony?" Cynthia asked, almost feverishly, "trying to make me lose?"

"Don't think so, just trying hard not to sin, because I know I'm a winner, baby."

"I feel ya," she said, grabbing hold of my manhood as I walked by.

"Don't get bit…"

"Bite me," she said, as I ran my hand up her thighs, journeying to the small of her back, letting my hand find its way to the nape of her neck, gently pulling her hair back as I began to kiss softly along the top of her bosom, moving along with patience and care, covering her with my desires, nibbling along the lobes of her ears, methodically dancing across her face with small, passionate filled kisses, before tenderly tugging on her tongue, forcing my own deep inside her mouth.

I still remember her smell and can taste her sweetness.

She was like putty in my hands, and I was determined to mold her the way I wanted.

The connection, passion and desire were so strong and so raw we barely made it to back to her place.

I still can't remember how we got through the drive, up the stairs and into her bed, but the journey was sweet and the rest is history…ancient history it seems sometimes, but not all the time, like now…

Drop
By
Drop

Ummm… that smells soo good… feels soo good;
sounds soo good; tastes soo good…
I wish I could, but I can't… Or Can I?...
Confusion?...   Or is it?...
Maybe I am… connected, recollected, faded out…
Back in again, to be lost, but somehow found…
Listening, feeling it falling down…
down…
down...
down…
Drop… by…
        Drop… by…
                Drop… by…
What a sound!
Catch it while you can…
'Cause when it's gone… it's gone?
Maybe so… you never know…

TL

For the pleasure, not the pain, I told myself as I worked out, trying to avoid having knee surgery, hoping to prolong and preserve myself, as my life seemed to take a course of its own.

She was independent, tough, sweet, mesmerizing, sexy, cautious, loyal, honest (too honest sometimes), and calculating. Damn, why did she have to be my ex-wife's best friend!? I thought. What luck! Meet the girl I knew, that I knew, that I knew was the one, at least at the time, and she really wasn't because there was tricky wrapping around her I couldn't get through unless I got tangled all up in her too. I couldn't afford that, not now! I yelled at myself.

So, I began pretending.

I pretended it was okay we were just friends.

I pretended it was just fine that we would never escalate beyond just closet lovers.

"It's okay," I kept telling myself, thinking I was in control.

Hell, I was still a Marine and Marines always get through, I told myself one sunny Saturday morning while shaving as I prepared myself to meet with Cynthia later.

We decided to do a trip into DC, disregarding what others may have to say about us being together. We're all adults, and sometimes life becomes a game of matching, and it's up to us as adults to make the best of our situations, we figured. It was cool with us, so it should be cool with our friends and family, we argued with confidence.

Before we made it into DC we had to take her car into the shop to check a suspicious noise she heard while driving. I first realized it wasn't at all cool with us at the shop. I had become her pseudo-man, accustomed to her wants and desires and she began needing me to be something more than her friend with benefits.

"Well, little lady, it's a shame you waited so long to bring your car in; it's gonna cost you a little bit more than what we advertised. Sorry," the mechanic said to Cynthia with a small chuckle.

"But, I didn't know, I just thought I could get it in when I could and it would be ok. My man didn't mention anything to me about it," Cynthia said while looking me up and down with a smirk on that pretty face of hers.

I just smiled and leaned back against the wall drinking my orange CRUSH purchased from the unusually loud soda machine facing away from the counter where Cynthia and the mechanic haggled.

"Whatever," I responded back. "You know how women are, man," I said to the overly greased mechanic. "Never tell you anything until it's too late," I continued with a chuckle of my own.

"Don't I know it," the mechanic said laughing. "My wife's the same way. It must be a woman thing."

"Not funny, not funny at all," Cynthia said with a look of hurt while sending vibes of her rage and change of mannerism fully toward me.

I took another swig of my soda pop and continued to smile, shaking my head, turning my attention out the window of the waiting room, thinking, boy, this sure feels weird. Why is she so mad? It's just a joke.

We were just cool, I thought to myself as we drove back to her place in silence, ditching our plans to hang out in DC, blaming it on the price of her car repair spoiling the mood. So she shouldn't be mad, right? I questioned, checking the information I had gathered and labored for thus far.

Besides, she was in a relationship or trying to end one that had cost her pain, suffering and humiliation physically, mentally, and emotionally. So I was a pressure release, to the say the least, I told myself as we motored out of the city toward northern Virginia.

I was just a relief valve but I still felt Naïve. Pathetic. Lost.

With a deep sense of humiliation, and the words of the stranger ringing in my mind, I turned to the only man I knew who had to know more about this love thing than me, my father. I called him and asked if I could come over and talk for a moment, promising not to take too much of his time away. He agreed. He had to deal with my mother at some point. He obviously failed, since they didn't last, but I felt that in the midst of whatever they had, he had to have learned something. I wanted to know what that something was.

"Hey Pops," I said, trying to make him feel like he had an enlightened status about him, a wisdom level I hoped to someday obtain, "tell me something, man, what's up with this woman thing? When I think it's all good and fun with them, I learn they want or need more. Then when I give them more, they tell me I'm too much or they wished 'we could just go back to being the way we were,'" I said, doing my best impression of the very words I heard from Cynthia only days before.

My dad started chuckling to himself which I found to be rude and obnoxious considering this was the first time we had managed to attempt such an open conversation since I first arrived in his world ten years before.

"Son, I told you awhile back during your first marriage that you won't ever be able to figure a woman out and she ain't gonna ever be able to figure you out. The best you can hope for is mutual consent to do each other good. But, as always, you don't listen to me. You wanna explore and conquer don't 'cha?" he said, laughing deep and low within his rounded belly, looking like a slimmed out Santa, decked with the glasses and all.

I looked at him while shaking my head, smiling.

"Man, I always listen to you, especially when you think I'm not. I just try to tweak what you say, you know, bring it to modern times."

He laughed at me even more.

"Boy, there ain't no modern times. It's all the same time, different looking space, but all the same. Your best bet is to be on the up as much as you can. Even when you ain't up, think up and get there."

"I am trying…"

"Stop trying and start being! It's all in what you make of it. Right now, I tell you what you're doing, you're walking out of one downed love into another one. You better at least enjoy the ride," he said, getting up from the kitchen table and walking toward his bedroom.

Did I even want love?

It seemed as though I was always searching to be someone's Knight in Shining Armor, the one in all the fairy tales. Although, my life was somewhat like one to me, making me think that in the end, if I wasn't careful, the dragon would slay me.

I had to have a drink, so I called up my man Ian, knowing I had to first get past his Mrs.

"Hey, what's up Tina, how are you?" I asked, after the phone was picked up on the first ring.

"Doing well Tony, where are you?"

"Oh, just out and about, trying to clear my head a bit. Was wondering if you would let Ian out. I could sure use his company," I said in a half joking, half complimentary way, knowing Ian would appreciate me telling him about it later.

"Well let me put him on the phone for you. You take care of yourself and don't keep him out too late."

"Cool. You're a sweet heart. Thanks."

My man, Ian confirmed my thoughts without me even saying a word to him as we sat at the bar sipping beer and shooting Tequila shots in Mulligans, a sports bar downtown in DC, while watching the Wizards get ran out the gym.

"Dude, check it out. You are free, brother, you have an excellent opportunity to mingle with some fine women, man, and do it in style. Why you even thinking of being with another girl seriously? Are you crazy?" he asked with a hint of irritation in his voice.

Since he was married, he looked at me as one of the last kats able to hold it down in the single category.

"Ian, you know I take care of business, but it's something about Cynthia, man."

"Yeah, you right, that something is ease and comfort. Watch yourself, partner, what seems good isn't always right, especially this one, man. You have it all in front of you, just go get it and watch your back, boy. It should be about you first; that's the only way you can make it right for another, and that's my word," he said. The jukebox kicked out Common's spirit filled lyrics "I Used to Love HER," filling the space in the background.

For a moment I grasped it all.

But only for a moment.

The next moment, she came, almost as perfect as sunshine, right into my head.

No need to flip the image, no need to squint or figure out who and why, because there she was.

I felt as though I had to at least try with her.

So I did.

I was trudging on dangerous grounds, willing to sacrifice all good intentions for moments of passion and feverish lust. I thought good sex was a great mind-altering drug, especially when coupled with what I expected to find in another.

"Cynthia, baby, I'm coming over," I said over my cell while speeding toward Arlington at 2 am, knowing full well I had to be at work in 3 hours. Not to mention there was a good chance her ex could be there as well, since he was trying to push himself back in the door.

I didn't care.

"Tony, I am dog-tired, boy, why are you calling me this late?" she said, groggily, as if she had been tossing and turning, unable to find comfort in her bed. Her voice made me want to disappear from my driving, then suddenly reappear next to her.

"I need to feel you, girl, right now," I moaned to her. "I will be there in 15," I said and hung up before getting a rejection.

I knocked on her door and as soon as she opened it, I began kissing her passionately until we melted to the floor with the door left standing wide open, exposing us as two lustful and wanting animals. I found one of my hands wandering along her thighs, while the other finger-tipped its way along her neck and face. She knew I wanted her badly.

"Tony," she gasped softly.

"Shh…I got this. You belong to me right now," I whispered.

I gently lifted her from the floor and walked back into her bedroom, nibbling on her ear and neck along the way, closing the door on her yelping little dog with my foot.

We found in each other the strength to laugh, play and wonder.

I brought to her the belief of spirituality beyond just self; she gave to me courage to question everything. We seemed to be yin and yang together, revealing the bountiful color saturation of black and white.

"You ever wonder why this, Tony? You know, why this way?" she asked me one night as we were lying in bed after a long game of hide and seek.

"Sometimes, but when I do, I always think up."

"What do you mean 'up'?" she said, sitting up on her elbows.

"Well, I always think that someday, you and I will be we."

She placed her head on my chest, and I could feel the cool but warm feeling of her breathing meeting the wetness of her tears. It seemed for the first time that we had actually made a step toward something out of nothing.

************Slow Rolling************

LovetsoL

Where is that sound coming from
So sweet and pure…
Where is that feeling of divinity
I missed for sure…
Why do I even tremble or cry
Out in pain galore…
Why is the sun setting
On my desires for sure…
What is it about this dance
That makes me lose my mind…
What do you mean stay awhile
Or love and loss I'll find…
Who will it be
To help this restless spirit be…
Who do I know or not know
Someone soft to behold
How will I know
If you're waiting in the wings…
How will I know
Listen to the humming bird sing…

TL

*************Slow Rolling************

dapt and overcome. I heard those words too many times, but yet in- still, here I was facing a double crisis. Fumbling with love again.

My health was causing a catastrophic break down in my life, picking annoyingly at my ca- reer and reason for being.

I distinctly remember her helping me through one of the toughest times of my life -- physical injury. Having blown out my knee, but instead of having surgery, I decided to contin- ue working hard at keeping my leg strong after transferring to Quantico, Virginia. I soon realized surgery was inevitable, and, along with my failing extremity that needed instant repair, my love crisis was worsening, seemingly un-amendable.

Cynthia took over in the welfare depart- ment, becoming a force for me in the most tur- bulent time of my existence.

Beep, beep, beep. I awake to. Slowly open- ing my eyes and seeing the smiling face of Cynthia looking down upon me.

"You did good," she said, squeezing my hand gently. "The doctors think you will be fine, once the swelling goes down."

"Can I get up now?" I asked foggily. "I feel like I been laying here forever."

"Tony, you just had surgery on your knee? Do you honestly think you can walk?"

"Yeah, I'm fine. I just needed to get up," I said throwing the covers back revealing my legs, one brown and hairy, and the other white as snow, heavily bandaged.

I didn't let the look faze me. I grabbed my wounded knee and swung it out over the edge of the bed and scooted forward toward the end.

Leaning forward and throwing my weight to the right, I felt pretty good about my chances of being able to walk again. As I rose to my feet, I slowly begin to feel my left leg give away, and before I knew it, I was smelling the lemon freshness of my laminated hospital room floor.

"Tony!" Cynthia yelled.

She picked me up off the floor with me laughing, easing here fear.

"Well damn, I guess I can't walk right now," I said as Cynthia helped me up.

"Will you please do both of us a favor and stop being a fool," she said, beginning to laugh with me.

"I'll try," I said, wiping of the sweat that was starting to drip down my face.

Cynthia was there beside me through all those times and more.

A time when I couldn't walk properly without keeling over in excruciating pain. A time when I was on my back for months, hardly able to place any weight on my failing extremity. A time when I felt sorry for myself.

"Damn! I can't make it up those fuckin' stairs, Cynthia; this shit hurts. I can't bend my knee enough. Every time I do it feels as though my leg is going to fall off," I moaned to her three days after the surgery while trying to make it up to her apartment on the fourth floor, a defeated man of war.

"All I hear you saying is what you can't do because of pain, when I know you can do this and much more. You just want to whine, don't you?" she fired back at me.

I tried to get mad.

I tried to catch an attitude.

I even tried to get up the stairs on my own.

She had me.

"See, what did I tell you? Here, baby, put your arm around my neck and let's get up those bad stairs," she said in a gentle, soothing, almost babying voice.

"You're a mess," I said, smiling at her but also at the situation.

I knew she was one-of-a-kind, someone who would have me through thick and thin and not give in and make me give up in hard times.

She was real.

She took care of me, watching over and motivating me to hit it hard to get back to the level I wanted.

But it was not to be.

The damage I had done to my knee during the pre-surgery years was extensive, causing much more damage than anyone had expected and destroying all the cartilage and severing the ACL from my bones. It was a devastating blow to me, one that rattled the shaky foundation of my inflated tough guy pride and ego; and jeopardizing any future developments to come with the Corps as well.

I was watching my break-up with the love of my manhood, my reason for rearranging my life, form right before my eyes, as the passing months of pain and rehab progressed, my impossible goals gave way to mere hopes of no longer wanting to wobble when I walked.

She was there.

I loved her and wanted her to be mine.

But she left.

She said she had to continue to chase her dreams, and no matter how much of a connection we had, it was not worth losing her fire, her passion, and her desires.

I agreed; hell, I was a Marine, I definitely understood.

"Death before dishonor, especially dishonoring you," I told her over the phone, coating my pain, giving thanks for not being in her presence as my mind began to scramble.

I followed her and began the show I had once performed so admirably in Alexandria with Sam, all over again.

It was a weird turn of events. One minute I was on the phone talking with her –

"Cynthia, I miss you, and I know I need you in my life."

"Tony, I miss you, too, but I can't. We have to do this, don't you know that?" she asked almost in a whisper. –

The next minute I was driving down the highway, headed toward an unknown, but determined to do something, anything to make it right.

"You're nothing! A nobody, just like your dad, just dead weight and you wonder why nobody loves you! It's because you're a nobody, boy! I should just kill you right now and put you out of your fucking misery," he gnarled, his upper lip curled as if disgusted about having his gorilla size hands wrapped around my neck as I stood tip-toed against the wall, searching for air with my toes, barely touching the cool feel of the concrete slab that sent a chill through my bones, relaxing me and making me go with the bliss of truth...I am a nobody...and it's okay to just be...

Suddenly my whole body felt the coolness of the concrete slab soothing me back into consciousness, and I realized I was still alive, a nobody with a permit to live a little more. I lay there and dreamt of the day when my grand- mother's words would come true, setting me free to love and be loved in return, because God said so...

Throughout the drive, which pushed my cran- berry-colored Mustang to its limits, I kept trying to get Cynthia on the phone to let her know I was coming to talk. Face-to-face.

I didn't get her.

I pulled in the small town of Eastern Shore, as the sun started to set over the trees adorning the roadside. I waited in a parking lot of a local grocery store. I had no idea where she lived.

"I know you live here somewhere," I found myself saying out loud, "now it's just a matter of where."

I was determined to see her that night, come hell or high water.

So I sat.

I watched as the cars in the parking lot upon my arrival slowly dwindled to none and the lights within the small grocer disappeared.

I listened to the hum of the parking lot lights come to life.

Finally, after two hours, she picked up the phone.

"Tony, why are you making this so hard? I am hurting just as much as you are, but I want to get over and through this," she said, sound- ing exasperated. "The timing for us just isn't right."

"I'm here in Eastern Shore, waiting in the parking lot of Highland Grocery, across from a set of railroad tracks...waiting for you," I told

her slow and patiently, so she could know I was
serious about us.

"You're what?"

"I've been trying to call and talk with you
for four or five hours now. I just needed to
see you one last time before we said goodbye."

"Tony…" she said trailing off. "I will be
there in a minute." She hung up abruptly.

I could tell she was irritated, but we had
to face-off at some point.

She came and escorted me from the parking
lot to her house, a little humble place surrounded by trees a few miles from campus,
enough for her and her dog.

We talked and soon became engrossed in one
another's lives again after having been out of
touch over the last few months, her with school
and me with the Corps.

"So, now what?" we asked simultaneously,
reading each other's energy, going with the
flow.

We vowed to make it work, again.

We had so much to share with one another
and so much to see together and so much joy to
bring to each other, we reasoned, forgetting
the tick, tock, tick, tock of time and the
emptiness of space.

Off again, on again Cynthia and I
went…finding salvation in The Word, losing
faith in words…slowly letting go of promises
that were obviously meant to be broken.

We shattered, again.

I was faced with the memory of signing on
the dotted line. I was lost in a sea of darkness, caught creating my manhood, guided by the
pure revelation that my heart, mind and spirit
belonged to the Corps, still.

I longed for the courage to face the storms
of my life.

I now understood why love hurts for a reason. And the rest is history, ancient history it seems sometimes, but not all the time, like now...

Variation of Time

Speckled as spots on mushroom tops,
Plentiful as the species of trees,
Boundless as the sky above,
Depthless as the ocean blue
Laid out as spring flowers are in a field,
Clumped together as seals lying on sandy beach
fronts,
Dirty as sticky brown mud,
Vibrant as the rising sun,
Full as a harvest moon,
Elusive as galloping antelopes,
Determined as pouncing cats,
Focused as approaching crocs,
Playful as monkeys, too,
Deadly as viral outbreaks,
Connected as lands once were
Re-connecting as lands will be
Exclusive as nothing is…
Humanity's Will…

TL

One of the wonderful things about being in the Marines were the places I was able to live, which I wouldn't have under normal circumstances, such as Oceanside, California.

My best friend, Bobby, thought the time I would spend in California would be beneficial. He envied me to some degree.

"Man, you're about to go where the women are golden, the night life is flamboyant and there is fun to be had on every turn, bro'. Do your thing man, do your thing," he said jovially, as though he were packing his things to tag along.

I knew this wasn't going to be just a joy ride. I knew there was lots of work to be done and plenty of time spent within the confines of four walls, but I knew the moment I felt the warm glow of Cali sun, I was going to go bananas.

"Yeah, bro', it should be love."

It seemed like yesterday, when I could see so clearly the way things would unfold, like yesterday when love was slowly and methodically forming yet another opportunity for me to see life in all of its splendor.

"I can't wait to get there, man," I told Bobby while I visualized long winding beaches with beauties as far as the eye could see.

He smiled as if he was seeing the same.

Bobby had the ultimate life, raised in a household with both parents, military kid, only child, cautiously raised and rendered, slowly and purposefully cared for by parents and friends alike. I wondered why he felt the way he did about me, someone trying to get by. He was the spawn of a balanced specimen, an all around good guy. So to have me as his best friend, a psychotic, schizophrenic, manic-depressive male in search of love was odd.

He just thought I was passionate about things, albeit a little crazy, he would say.

What else could he need? I thought as I finished packing my things.

I was getting the itch again to go and test my healing knee.

"Let's go ball man," I said, turning to Bobby, firing the ball towards his chest I had just picked up from the floor.

"Bet," he responded, catching the ball with one hand before it hit him in the face.

Being a baller like me, Bobby was an athletic type who loved to converse with the rock in his hand, and I was happy to join him.

Even though I now had a surgically prepared left knee, I knew I needed the strenuous motion of poetic exercise, basketball. I loved the feel of control, taking my shots whenever, deciding where and how they would land.

"What's up with you and Cynthia, partner? I know you done hit that right?" he asked me while trying to take me to the hole.

"Come on, B, you know I can't tell. I'm a gentleman. But she is sweeeet," I said, laughing out loud while going for the block.

"Man, you a gigolo, about to invade Cali! Watch out now!" he joked, as I swished a jump shot in response.

"Bro', I'm just trying to be happy. I feel like I have spent a huge part of my life trying to make others happy at my expense. It's getting old, B," I said, taking a break to look out into the darkening woods that loomed behind the court separating the two neighborhoods where Bobby and I grew up.

It reminded me of simpler times.

"Shit, I hear you. Sometimes you have to love 'em and leave 'em, man, and you know that's the truth," he said, leaning on my shoulder as we both watched the sun as it began disappearing through the trees.

"Specially you, bro', you been through the fire. It's only right you play. But be smart man…be smart," he said while backing me down under the lights of our boys-to-men playground.

I walked away from the court with Bobby, feeling a little bit more empowered and justified. Basketball still seemed to have magical powers for me, taking away some of my pain, but I still felt empty, without knowing why...just plain empty.

Cali and duty called, and of course, I answered, newly repaired knee and all.

I felt as though I was made to enjoy 'em and love'em all.

From crooning to ladies on a beach front through an open window to dazzling them with tailored suits and fake VIP's in hot nightclubs throughout San Diego, I did it all.

Cali was love.

In the midst of running from Los Angeles to Tijuana, I developed a good relationship with a fellow male Marine, Daiyon. We called him the Disciple, because he was known for handing out the gospel of womenology. Through many conversations over Capt-n Coke while watching the ladies dance to Tupac Shakur, we decided we needed to hook up a place when we got back home and install revolving doors for our women.

One weekend all the fellows decided to barbeque and invite our newly forming harem of women over to enjoy the warm weather and good food.

I fancied myself a master chef, so we did it up, talked it up, ate it up and drunk it up.

"Cali, cali, cali, what a place to be, money. Got my man T on the grill, the honeys coming through and the drinks all chill. Yeah, man, this is love," Daiyon boasted.

"What's cool, man, is we got a chance to do this and keep it tight between us, 'cause we all know how it goes when girls come around and kats want to act like they have to protect their shit. This is love…for real," I said.

"Damn, T, you getting all deep on us, bro'. What's up, you getting soft, dude?" Raul asked sarcastically.

"Man, I am just acknowledging the fact that we can do this shit, with no problems, no drama and no fear, you feel me? Besides, I got your soft, step up if you wanna, I'll still put you on your back, partner," I said, flexing my right arm, making my bicep jump out, pointing to it with the barbeque fork. "Don't let the smooth taste fool you, bro'," I said with a chuckle.

Everyone just laughed and toasted to good times.

"T man, you're definitely an original," Raul said.

This was the ultimate liberation. No more worries or concerns over finding true love, I thought to myself as I lay in bed that night, basking in the events of the day. Nothing's true anyway. Love is overrated and unobtainable and I was glad I found out sooner rather than later.

My thoughts danced, falling back and forth into a sea of illusion. I was still young, I thought, convincing myself further that my whole makeup was about instant pleasure. I became a walking pleasure seeker and was loving it...

As with most maniacs, my highs didn't last forever, and a few days later I eventually found myself back down in the hole of depression and questioning everything once again.

Why this?

Why me?

Why now?

Why be?

The same old questions I pondered, revealing the absolute of nothingness, forging my desire to want somethingness.

Cali-love ended as quickly as it began.

Sitting in my room back in Woodbridge, Virginia, in the newly ordained House of Marine Whores, I realized something was missing.

Even after sharing a night of passion and a day of vertical and horizontal exercises with a fine lady of cocoa butter skin, I realized something more must exist, cause this wasn't it.

I had pushed my life out of context, leaving me feeling upside down.

I went and knocked on the door of the co-captain of the House, Daiyon, with the sounds of Nina Simone version of "My Baby Just Cares For Me" coming through his door, and he told me I needed more women.

"Variety is the key," he said.

He instructed me on keeping my feelings separate from my desires, keeping my passion away from my wants and keeping my big head apart from my little one.

He was truly a master of deception and a keeper of the code of womanizing, something I quickly realized I wanted no part of, no matter how soft the feel of silky-smooth thighs was or how vibrant the sounds of a passionate moan may have been.

I knew I needed more…

I longed for Cynthia. I hadn't seen or talked with her since going and coming back from California, and after 6 months of excluding her from my mind, she came crashing back into it.

So, I called, rekindled, reenacted and resurrected our love affair again, just to see it fizzle to nothing.

Pour on the depression, this time add a little fear.

Fear of being alone, fear of not living up to the standard of being a man, fear of not hearing the sounds of a little one made from love, fear of not having someone to grow old with (like Cynthia and I said we would), fear of not having found my purpose in life, fear of losing at the game of life, fear of never reaching my potential, fear of loathing, fear of being...FEAR stared me down, revealing to me that god had found no favor thus far in my being.

Then she came…and the rest is history, ancient history it seems sometimes, but not all the time, like now…

The Moments of Fascination in Grandeur

Inspired by the very look in your eyes,
Fulfilled by the essence of togetherness,
Embracing; changing as the wind blows free,
Knowing certainly the way it should be,
Only time tells, reveals, uncovers and heals,
Really! Are you for real?
Striking, like words from on high,
Listening refocuses the moments before they die,
Holding true to those precious things,
Understanding; processing, while breathing…it stings –
Space… how empty it seems…
Inspired by the melody of trees,
The smell, the taste, the feel of it all,
How wonderful it is to fall!
Triumph over your greatest fear,
Stand tall… shhhh… can you hear?
Uncluttered at last, the time is near,
Full speed ahead, now brace yourself,
Down again, do you need some help?
Open your eyes, the best is yet to come,
Dance on under the rising sun,
Fluid as a river flows,
There she goes…

TL

Growing impatient with the dullness of multiple lovers, I decided to try abstinence. This translated to lots of working out at the gym, playing ball for the relief of pressure and working long hours to try and satisfy my need for another's touch.

Having met lots of people, both men and women alike, who believed it was godly for a man to find a wife, I had multiple friends looking out for my The One, and she supposedly like working out in the same gym as the wife of one of my fellow Marines.

"Hey, T," I Michelle called to me as I walked to my car after a long day of military politics.

"Hey, what's up girl? Long time, no see. Robert got you locked away again?" I teased.

"You know better than that!" she fired back. "Anyway, I met this young lady at the gym last night, and I think she is right up your alley."

"Excuse me, up my alley? And what is that supposed to mean? You talking slang to me, girl," I joked.

"Boy, don't play with me," she said, showing that attitude Robert talked about loving so much.

"Well," I continued, "how does she look?"

"I wouldn't throw you any garbage; plus, she works out, so you know she got it together."

"I hear ya. I tell you what, give her my number and tell her to hit me up then. What you waiting for girl? Don't make me get Ruddy on you," I said as I walked away, chuckling to myself.

"Boy, please!" she answered with a frown. "See you later, and you better answer your phone when she calls. I know you,"

"Got'cha'," I yelled as I jogged off to my car, trying to get away from the match-maker, not really concerned or excited at the thought of meeting another woman.

And I definitely wasn't sprung on the idea of meeting a female Marine through a hookup. Male Marines loved to pass rumors expressing the unattractiveness, good for fun and nothing more, and tendency to jump in the bed with every male Marine they saw nature of women Marines. Consequently, I had never looked in that direction for any form of pleasure.

But, the connection was made immediately.

"Hello is this Tony?" I heard the whisper of my fantasy come rushing back in again over my phone.

"Speaking. Who's this?"

"Missy, your friend gave me your number and I was wondering aloud to myself, do you realize it would have been better received if delivered in person," she said. I couldn't tell if she was being serious, rude, playful or all the above.

So I said, "Not really. I didn't expect to hear from you, if you want to know the truth. But, now that you've called, I think it's only fair if you tell me what you're wearing," with silence coming from the other end of the line. "Come on girl, don't get shy on me now. Remember you called me, proving to me you have moxy, mojo or you're one tough cookie. Which is it? Tell me now, but first, what are you wearing?" I said jokingly, trying to lighten the mood, while letting her know she had be quick.

CLICK.

I soon heard the sound of the dial tone in my ear and I began to laugh.

I hit redial and she picked up on the first ring.

"Is that enough moxy for you?" she asked. "Please don't be typical. I'm not," she said with a hint of cynicalness in her voice.

"Let's do dinner and see," I fired back at her.

"Tomorrow at 6:30 in front of your office."

"Bet," I said.

I met her around 7, expecting and preparing myself for a shocking hoochie-mama, hood-rat, crazy-girl with no sense. When I first laid eyes on her, I saw a sparkle that seemed to ignite a fire of want in me.

I had to get to know her.

She was dressed in a light blue spaghetti-strapped sundress that flowed outward at the bottom. Her hair was curled and hanging down, barely touching the top of her dress.

"You're Missy?" I asked, a little choked up from what my eyes were processing.

"Last time I checked I was," she said in a sweet and playful voice. "And you must be Tony?"

"I think so, but right now I'm caught up here in wonderment." I said, feeling a little under-dressed in my kaki slacks and white button down.

"Why is that?" she asked, a smile forming on her face.

"Well, last time I checked works of art and beauty didn't come to life, especially on a Marine base."

"Why thank you. You're not so bad yourself," she responded with a smile, without appearing to be overly moved by my comment.

"Well, let's go eat, before I eat you," I
said, giving her a wink, opening the car door,
helping her inside.

"You're so cheesy," she said, giggling as
she made herself comfortable in the front seat
of my Mustang, a true to life doll with tiny
dimples on both sides of her face and deep
brown eyes immersing me in the rivers of her
bottomless bliss.

It was amazing how my mind could rearrange
my thoughts just by romancing my eyes. Beauty
always triumphs over rationale for me, every
time.

We laughed and talked through dinner alongside the Potomac River at a small Italian restaurant tucked away and lightly lit enough to
evoke moods of a romantic and playful nature. I
saw visions of past loves showing glimpses of
themselves in the subtlety of her words and the
gentleness of her tone. The charm was poured on
thick by both sides, a revelation slipping in
from time to time, as a hook to pull us closer
together, both wanting to know more and more
about one another.

We drove back to her place in a fog of nos-
talgia basking in its coolness, continuing our
talk and laughter inside of her dorm barracks
room located to the east of the air field, with
shadows of helicopters darting along the edge
of the runway.

Our first date was an all nighter.

"Missy, I sincerely can say, this has been
one of the most enjoyable times in my waking
adult love life," I said to her that night.

"You're flattering me, Tony, although, I
have to agree with you. This is pretty cool,
and who would've thought with a male Marine.
You know the reputation you guys have is pretty
shitty," she said with a snicker.

We both began to laugh.

"So, where do we go from here?" I asked, rather anxiously.

"Well, considering it's six in the morning, I suggest you go home and I get in bed," she said.

"So witty but true. You're making me think about things differently, and for that I don't know whether to thank you or spank you," I responded with a smile.

"Maybe later. Good morning to you," she said, opening her front door to see me out.

"And to you as well," I said while shading my face from the glow of the rising sun.

"Damn, what a view, a new dawning," I said as I started singing Stevie Wonder's hit "That Girl" while bouncing to my car.

She stood in the door laughing at me.

"Boy, you're a piece of work."

"Don't I know it," I said before getting in the car and driving away.

After that first encounter, I talked to her at least five times a day and made it a point to see her at least three times a week, regardless of what the Corps demanded.

What a ride, what a thrill, what a blind side flying tackle that felt so good it seemed it couldn't hurt.

My life began to feel like a dream again, captivating and transmogrifying me, and I felt as though I needed to wake up. I tried to convince myself, but to no avail.

After several months of spending time at her place or mine together, it struck me very concretely.

Meeting Missy had to be heaven sent, and I was going to test the validity of it by ignoring her.

Such wonderful logic, coming from a smart man, I thought to myself, but maybe it'll work, reverse order logic.

"Dude, we have got to get the hell out of here, Daiyon. I am losing it man. Look at me, bro', I am falling head over heels here. This wasn't supposed to happen," I said one evening shortly after Missy left to head home.

"What about Cali, man? Wasn't that just a few months back?"

"Chill, kat, I got you. Let's go to the Chi', the ladies and love there will bring your ass back. I promise you that," he said cool, calm and collected.

Three C's I definitely was not.

We steamed to Chicago, getting there half a day later. It was a great time, but I kept thinking of the lady back in Virginia.

Missy had to be the one, I was certain, because here I was in the Windy City, chasing dimes and quarters, laying foundations, but constantly thinking of her. Thinking of the night we stayed up all night and talked about anything from nothing, reminiscing on the good old days of house parties and fades, exploring the endless possibilities of the future, where we would be in 10 years, 20 years, after death… what a perfect moment in time.

We found ourselves speeding back from Chicago a day early, just so I could tell her I wanted to make her mine.

"Daiyon, man, we have to go bro', I need to get back and take care of some business."

"I promise you, T, she will be there when you get back, no doubt," he said, seeing right through me.

"Naw, man, it's not even like that," I began defending myself, knowing damn well I had been read. "I just gotta handle a few things."

"Yeah, I feel ya," he said, crossing his eyes at me under the brim of his cap. "I feel ya."

"Whatever, let's go, fool," he said, jumping into the passenger side as we zoomed back East.

Twelve hours later, 3:00 a.m., mission accomplished, I started to have doubts while lying with her under the light of a full moon.

Was this true, right, and sincere?

I decided to relax and enjoy the moments as they came, knowing good and well the next one would not be guaranteed, and, if it did happen, it could be a bad one.

We blossomed, while my time in the Marine Corps became even more challenging thanks to my failing body. Because of my serious knee issues, the Corps began to have a problem with our relationship.

I went from being the honored son to the expendable, useless one. My heart mattered not, and the last rip of dignity and respect for my original plan, life and accomplishments came falling down.

"Brown, I don't know if it would be a good idea for us to promote you right now," SgtMaj Bottom said to me one day during a closed door, one on one meeting, after it was discovered I was up for promotion to the next higher grade, despite being injured.

"Why's that SgtMaj? I mean I've done all that's required to be promoted. Although I've been hurt, I still give my all and compete well."

"Well, that's just it. In the Corps, we don't promote broken bodies. A broken body takes up space, preventing someone else from getting ahead as well."

"With all due respect, SgtMaj, this broken body out-performed almost all of your healthy bodies. Don't you think I deserve some recognition for that?" I asked, a little agitated.

"True as that may be, Brown, I am going to recommend passing you up until you get fixed. That's all."

"But SgtMaj…"

"That's all, Corporal!" he barked.

My always come first love was done loving me.

She was there.

"Missy, what the hell am I gonna do? I love the Corps and have always loved the Corps. What the hell!" I yelled out that night while lying in bed with tears running down my face.   "I have never been loved," I said softly, taking in the last burns of a life that seemed like a distant memory, ablaze and roaring, blowing the residue of forgotten times in my eyes.

"Baby, it's alright," she said, while rubbing my chest, "life goes on and just maybe it's your time to get onboard another train and head in a different direction. Besides, I love you."

"Yeah, but I'm not ready to leave…I'm just not ready, yet."

"Well, sometimes you're ready and you don't even know it. Change can be scary, but at the same time and in the same breath, it could be your only friend, too."

Those words seemed to linger in the air as I stared them down, not wanting to accept the strength of their truth.

The truth hurts, I thought.

I gathered those words and placed them in my heart, knowing they would go forth with me from that day on. I knew Missy was legit.

I recalled the words of my grandmother again that evening, *"Baby, God has put his anointing on you. He wants you to carry his message to and fro', Tony, because he has found favor in you and how you make His words cleanse others' fears."*

Eventually I got promoted, after some politicking with my boss, LtCol Weimer, who put pressure on the situation, but my days were numbered and my heart ached from the pain of rejection and the looming falling axe.

I wanted so badly to remain committed to my love, the Corps.

I began talking to my boss about the possibilities of sticking around, working for the Lab, anything to stay.

Although he was a big towering man who looked as though he didn't have a soft spot within an inch of his body, LtCol Weimer was more than willing to get me in a position to stick around. He generously began writing the job description for me to become a civilian worker in the Lab.

"The realistic side here, Sergeant Brown, is the fact that no matter what I say and how much I push, your time as an active duty Marine is just about done. Do I think that you can still go? You're damn right I do, but rules are rules. Now if you want to still be a part of the Corps, this is the way to go, and I know you would be an excellent fit. So, what do you say?"

This was it…the ultimate position to be in, the ability to take it to another level with this love thing of mine, and yet I stuttered.

"Sir, can I give it some deeper thought and let you know soon?"

"Sure, take your time. I understand."

My dilemma, coming around full circle, once again. From beginning to end, the game of love always has curves, I thought, walking out of LtCol Weimer's office.

I wanted this like no tomorrow.

But there was still the matter of Missy.

She was ready to leave the service and had planned to go back home to Illinois. She wanted me to come with her.

"Tony, I love you. You have to come. I don't want to lose you, and I know you feel the same."

My heart was criss-crossed and my mind was doing back flips, and lord knows where and what my spirit was doing. I could only stare out the window of the two-bedroom apartment we had lived in together for 6 months.

Again, the dilemma of choosing between a female love and the Corps stared me in the face.

"Marry me, Tony. Why don't we just get married?" she said. "We love each other and that's all we need."

"No, it isn't all we need; we need a view too," I responded.

"Which is why moving and going out to the Midwest makes perfect sense," she responded. "Let's get married, pregnant and start a new life together, Tony."

My mind sped up 10 times and my heart seemed to have exploded. Marriage? A baby? New life? It all seemed surreal and challenging, I thought as I sat staring at the old creaky tree in the backyard. It looked solid, swaying along to the rhythm of the wind, singing its song of longevity, never breaking away from its tune of desire to live long and strong. I looked up at Missy and saw her anticipation. I saw her longing, and her wants and could identify with her need to be loved. I saw a chance at chasing happiness in a new arena with a woman I loved. I saw a slice of homemade pie so perfectly made it could make me cry. I caught a glimpsed at the essence of love, again.

"I mean does it get any clearer than this? I love you, and I would do anything to make you happy, and I have known this for quite sometime. Honestly, I didn't expect to be here again, not this soon, not this way, and not with you. I never imagined finding myself in someone else. I never imagined I had the desire to sacrifice again…until you. You revealed in me all the holes I had concerning love. You know my flaws. You fill them. You even know my pain, my weaknesses, my fears, and self-destructive, panic filled rage of desire to succeed and be something, to prove that I do exist! And yet you still remained. You know my ups; you know my downs, my cries for justice in a seemingly unjust world and, it has to be you…" I trailed off staring into her eyes, captivated by my words. A sudden feeling of bliss in love filled my very being.

I fell to my knees and took Missy's hand, kissing her fingers, her wrist, and her forearm until her hand rested upon my chest. Looking into her eyes, I knew what I must do.

"Missy, I am honored and in awe of the beauty of you, from your feisty nature to your

loving and warm charm, and I feel I should be
asking you to marry me."

She jumped on top of me in glee, forcefully
pushing her tongue down my throat as she pulled
my face closer, trying to merge us into one as
our bodies settled in a heap on the floor. I
held her as we tangled and kissed for what
seemed like eternity, running our hands all
over each other, making one another feel whole.

"For real?" she moaned afterwards.

"Yes, for real. I love you and I want to
make you happy for the rest of my days."

"I love you, too, Tony."

"You'd better," I said, beginning to tickle
her all over.

With newness all around, the pieces seemed
to just fall into place, and it felt right.

Off with the Corps, the hell with staying
committed. Take the job and shove it, sir, with
all due respect. I had to start fresh, with a
new love, a new outlook and a new passion.

That day in July was a hot one for Virginia. A courthouse appearance, Missy dressed in
crème, me dressed in light green, tears flowing, time standing still, and the rest is history… ancient history it seems sometimes, but
not all the time, like now…

Burnt Words

Smoldering away, tearing at your spirit with
a force of tremendous glow
Undying pressure slowly causing tears to flow
Why? you ask as the words linger but soon fall away
Forever, it seems, they fade into the dark abyss
of nothingness...
It comes upon you so fast, full of fury, full of pain
The moments twisting and turning - ripping and burning
Get Away! Get Away! your heart exclaims
But you know, it is all for gain
Through the fire one must go
If one is to grow, it must be done slow...
But those words, those awfully formed, contorted words...
Leaving a scar that will forever remain
Branding you with love; making you insane
Or so you think, but is it so...
The world may never know...

TL

We left the Corps, vowing to love each other for life. We packed up our belongings and began the long and tedious journey across the mountains and hills of Pennsylvania toward Illinois, with plans for Missy's dream wedding formed, so the whole world would know she was hitched and pregnant.

Getting married a second time was strange and disconcerting for several reasons.

First, I had vowed to never do it again, unless an act of god set it up.

Secondly, no one knew I had taken the plunge, at least no one close to me, which in a way gave even more credence to our newfound discovery - disconcerting. All of my loved ones, adopted family and friends, loved her, and thought we were a great fit, but no one expected marriage - strange.

Third, although one half of me felt guided by this move as if it was not my will, as if I would be neither happy nor sad, fulfilled nor emptied, right nor wrong in anything that was to take place during our marriage.

I felt guided by commitment.

But, I also felt the influence of my thoughts rushing in and attacking the other half, leaving me feeling empty from the very same things that made me feel whole.

I soon became frustrated.

Frustrated because of the reality of Missy revealing the rawness of her first time being married and not knowing what to expect. Coupled with my relentless behavior and attitude toward perfection in love, it became a concoction for combustion. Frustration grew even more when we arrived on Missy's stomping grounds. Reality began to expose the truth.

Our union shared an embrace with desperation, filling the scene of our everyday life together with agony. We tried to stay afloat in a sea of faulty promises, held together by our mutual and yet separate desire for love.

Trying to please, trying to love anyhow, trying to be a friend, trying to be grounded in the midst of uncertainty, trying to be smart but humble, trying to be loving and gentle, trying to show we cared, trying everything, but failing miserably from the start.

In the back of my mind a hum became a whisper, as sweet as the one in which my fantasy of a lady love came true, a whisper begetting the question of why?

The first crash came within months of moving to the small city in Central Illinois, an old farming and fading industrial town set in its ways, avoiding any acts of sudden change and growth. Less than three months into her pregnancy we lost the baby.

Many things could have been blamed for this devastating blow, but I immediately started shouldering the blame, trying to take away Missy's pain. I stewed over my desperate search for a job in a town littered with bits of opportunity, and saw that I added more stress to our arrival from the moment we touched down. I made myself believe this, until it hurt me to look at Missy in her fallen state of grief.

As a prideful Marine, I was uncomfortable with having to live with her family until we got on our feet. I voiced this with her on every turn, multiplying her disillusionment with life and causing her more pain.

I found myself caught between moments of translation one evening, trying to recall life for us at that point. While strolling through the grocery store, bypassing the aisle stocked with baby products, everything seemed strategically placed just to mock me.

Numerous arguments began forming in my mind, mounting her against me from the start. And of course, leading to her family rallying against me, I reasoned with myself.

Leaving the confines of the store behind, after picking up bread and beer, I felt justified with my thoughts forming anger by the coldness of the wind that greeted. My stance and point of view solidified.

I became overwhelmed.

I felt trapped.

I began forming a wall, leaving Missy on the other side.

I just wanted away from the pain which caused an even stronger build up of animosity between the two of us.

From the start I wanted my wife to stand beside me, to get moving on accomplishing our collective goals and the individual ones we had agreed upon prior to making our trek across the Midwest. I wanted to place emphasis on us joining forces in the world.

"Baby, it's ok," I told Missy, "at least we still have each other, and maybe it wasn't meant for us to have children right now, you know?" I said to her one evening as we walked in the park, trying to spend some alone time together to work on patching the visible rift growing between us.

"No, I don't know. You have no idea what this feels like, Tony. And you just can't smooth it over as if it's gonna be okay. So don't even bother."

So, she has been building too, I thought.

"Missy, I am not trying to smooth it over; I'm just saying I'm here for you."

Silence…how deafening. It pierced like glass, and I was bleeding from the heart.

We soon found out the main cause of the miscarriage had more to do with procedure, life deciding to fly, not from the fight of our existing together as one.

I thought many nights, lying in bed, looking out at the darkening sky, our life seemed unnatural; our dying commitment hopelessly dead from the start.

We were hurting and clung to each other as a last sliver of hope of easing our pain.

I tried to be the one for her.

She was my wife and I loved her.

I tried desperately to shake off the devastating memories and my inability to forgive myself for not being strong enough to keep them at bay.

Missy no longer want to talk, walk or be with me.

I was getting tired.

I felt compelled to think of alternative plans, to exit stage left, since I was no longer wanted, needed or appreciated.

I called my man, Bobby, constantly for reassurance, seeking outside advice, looking for validation.

"Dude, it seems to me you're doing all you can, not to mention the fact that you left everything and everyone behind to be with her in the first place. Shit, she should be grateful. You're a good man, Tony, and a much more agreeable one than most! I would have never done what you did for no one, not even my momma!" he said, in a phone conversation one rainy Saturday evening, after one of about 200 blowups I had recently had with Missy.

We both laughed out loud, knowing good and well Bobby would go to hell and back for his momma.

"Which is part of your problem anyway," he said to me, "you need to stop spoiling your women."

He only spoke of what he saw.

What he did not see was that I chose to be what I was for Missy in response to her life of longing for love. As a child she wished only to be the apple of her absent father's eye. I connected with her, vowing to be her love and more.

Yet, I had failed her so many times.

"B man, I am tired bro'; something has to give. I don't know what else I'm suppose to do. I keep asking myself, why do I keep putting up with her? Then I answer my own damn question with another question of why would I quit loving her. But, I know something has got to give," I said to Bobby.

I visualized a miraculous transformation occurring within Missy's and I relationship.

I hoped for divine intervention.

I didn't want to lose out on love again.

Missy and I had been together for less than two years and now fostered a disdain for one another time couldn't even seem to heal.

Like a dart to the bulls-eye, love was to my heart.

Cynthia re-entered the scene, and my mind went into overdrive, outpacing my heart.

I saw the void that had not been filled, for either of us, and my emotions came flooding back in, tangling with my thoughts and endor-phanizing my actions.

Somewhere in between California and Mary-land Cynthia and I made a commitment to marry one day, and I'll be damned if she didn't take it to heart. Even after finishing school, mov-ing to Arizona and starting her career as an Industrial Engineer for Arizona's school sys-tems, she still wanted me.

And I still had deep-rooted feelings as well, I thought to myself as I pulled up into the driveway leading to my home one day after leaving work.

Cynthia, had traveled back home to D.C., caught up with Bobby for lunch and decided to slide him her number, hoping to have me call so we could catch up for old times' sake.

Bobby knew the problems I was having with Missy and that I had begun planning our di-vorce. Since he and I had discussed what seemed like my only option at the time, he decided he would help provide a little sunshine in the darkness of my crumbling reality.

"Cynthia, baby, long time, no hear from," I crooned over the phone the first night I called. I was locked up at work, guarding the inmates as they slept, confined in their cells.

"How have you been?"

"Why didn't you tell me you had gotten mar-ried and left? Why didn't you call or write or something?" she began, catching me off-guard, almost causing me to choke on the sudden compression of excitement and anticipation I had expected to hear in her response.

"Wait, wait, wait. Hold on for a second, Babe. I thought you were done with me, with us, and had moved on with your life. I did the same. I was just calling to see how you were and..."

"Yea, you did, with quickness too!" she said, sounding hurt, angry, offended and wishful all at the same time. "The truth is, I miss you, even when I thought I was done, knew I was done. I still missed you."

Something seemed to have sparked within her, a challenge to win back a prize. A game had begun, and I was a willing but unknowing participant.

In my eyes this was no big deal. My wife didn't care for me as she once had. She couldn't even look me in the eye and tell me she loved me anymore. If she did love me, I mattered very little in her world.

Cynthia was halfway across the country, living her life of success, her goals accomplished and her mind constantly challenged, her fear of failure extinguished, while mine continued to roar on.

For the first time I could see parts of myself trying to become whole. I began to understand why I had to endure certain tragedies in my young life.

"What happened?" a voice shook through me while I was rolled down a hallway with medical equipment on both sides, blinding lights pouring down from above me, all while blurred images behind masks that kept questioning me.

"What happened?" I turned my head to the left and realized someone was holding my hand and explaining to the images behind the mask how I was found, belt wrapped around my neck and tied to the bed, an empty bottle of Atenolol falling from my hand.

"I know my baby wouldn't hurt himself like this." It was my grandmother. "I told Linda that man was going to kill him if she didn't get him out of there." She sounded loud and upset, but at the same time faint to me, as we burst through a set of double doors. And then I blacked out again.

I awoke with a feeling of lightheadness. I couldn't tell if it was from the cathartic smell of my surroundings or from the throbbing emptiness I felt, swirling back and forth in a dense fog of pain. The metallic taste filling my mouth only intensified the darkness, leaving my eyes feeling as though they had been poked by two giant thumbs, provoking the light streaming down from above me to burn my deeply imbedded spirit.

I heard the voice of my grandmother whisper in my ear. "God has put his anointing on you, baby, you will always be healed." She rubbed my forehead, whispering those same words over and over again.

Unfortunately, Missy was directly affected by my new state of being. She felt something and began preparing herself for battle, to defend the sacredness of our false words, said out of hope, now drenched in reality. Suddenly she was trying hard to redeem the essence of our lost love.

It became evidently clear to me how Missy viewed us and our union in terms of love. When I thought it was okay to try and remove myself from her, she began acting as though I was the greatest thing ever to her, for her, by her.

"Hey baby, how was you night? Missy asked me one morning as I walked through the door, wiry and wired after a night of confusion and conversation with Cynthia, while half-heartedly performing my work assignments.

"It was okay," I responded dryly, trying to avoid having any contact with her for fear that she may find out that I had allowed Cynthia back into my world, jeopardizing our made up one.

"What's wrong with you?" she said, getting agitated, quickly exulting the tension between us.

"Shit Missy I'm tired as hell. I been up all night and frankly I don't get why you're coming at me as if you care. Why you fronting? Let's just stop playing fucking games with one another. That's what's wrong," I snapped, walking out of the doorway entrance where I felt I had been trapped and exposed, showcasing all my guilt.

"Well fuck you too then Tony. You're such an ass."

"Likewise," I said, slamming the bedroom door behind me, feeling some relief after getting her off my back for a while.

But Missy had passed through the healing phase of time, dealing with her loss the best way she could, and realized I was still around,. She had invested too much of herself, searching desperately for love, in such a short amount of time to sit back and watch a piece of herself fly away.

So she stayed.

I began speaking to one of my fellow co-workers about my situation. He was a burly but smooth, mature gentleman with the voice of God, and a sure command of space. He had the presence of a chiseled, gentle giant, and all the ladies loved him. His name was David Dunabi.

"I may be married, Tony, but I ain't blind and I sure can still smell, and, if I am feeling real good, I can even taste. That there," he said to me nodding his head in the direction of a fellow C.O. whose uniform grabbed hold of her body with an extra closeness, commanding everything within her circle of influence to pay attention, "is the greatest creation the good Lord ever made, but it's also the deadliest."

"Amen to that, brother," I said, shaking my head at the sight of such beauty and the truthfulness of Dave's words. "Let me ask you something, Mr. D. How do you handle a blast from the past coming back into your life when you and your wife are on the ropes?" I asked, knowing the response would be simple and pure.

"You don't. You let it slide right on through as if it's just that, your past," he said, looking at me with intensity. "Do you hear me, young man? Don't get caught up into that. I am telling you, it'll burn ya."

"Yea…yea, I hear ya Mr. D, I hear ya," I said.

I heard, but I wasn't feeling him. I felt there was something missing from his words of warning, a void of some sort he didn't even know he had left unuttered, and I had to find out what it was that left me feeling empty and overwhelmed.

Still, I took some of Dave's advice, unable to find the courage to probe further than where I had already gone with Cynthia.

I explained to her why nothing would or could become of us and that I had made a commitment to my wife, with the music of Marvin Gaye's Here My Dear album seeping through the catwalk from Mr. D's pod where he watched over his inmates.

"I married Missy for better or worse, and even though right now it seems we're getting a whole lot of worse, I love her still. And you know what they say Cynthia, 'love conquers all'," I said, to the mounds of silence on the other end of the line. "We had our chance, baby, and for that I will forever be thankful. It's because of you I still believe."

I received not even a murmur of a reply.

My belief that words make people feel love began to waver in the wind, ripping away from the foundation, from the true essence of my prophecy.

"Cynthia, baby, you know I love you and I can't ever stop that. But I can't go down that road again with you. Look where you and I are now, shit, not to mention Missy. She deserves better."

"Tony, I am not asking you to leave your wife for me. I am asking you to ask yourself why you're with her," she said. "But it's cool, I understand. I guess love does conquer all, even foolishness." I envisioned her letting the phone fall from her fingers to the waiting charging base, sending the tone of nothingness to my ears. Her words had been spoken from over 400 miles away, but they whispered again in my ear like the sound of an angel's wing swooping past my outstretched heart, reverberating through my spirit and transfixing my mind.

"Damn, damn, damn," I screamed while pounding my fist against the table, feeling like I was totally losing control of my tattered life.

I had to get it together, I thought, sitting in the dark, unconcerned about the inmates locked away below me.

Once again I pledged my faith, trust and loyalty to Missy alone, wanting to right the wrongs, push away the pain of our indecision and build on our experience of knowing where we didn't want to be… and the rest is history… ancient history it seems, sometimes, but not all the time, like now…

Perpetual Motion

Why not me, why not you,
These words, those things,
Making it hard, oh so hard,
Quietly waiting, silently looking,
Never knowing, but always asking,
This time it will flow,
This time it will last,
This time…

TL

issy and I began working on our marriage again, with an intent on starting the family we both wanted so badly to believe in.

"This will be a wonderful new start for us," Missy said to me, reaching over and squeezing my hand one early April morning as we sat in traffic, trying to leave Chicago, after having seen a specialist to assess our needs and chances of success in our new endeavor.

"Anything to make you happy, Missy. You deserve it," I said. Missy had grown up rough, and elements of her life reflected more pain than gain. I could relate to her, and pieces from our childhood bonded us like glue. She had lived through a childhood as hard as mine, hoping to one day be loved for life, and she was still learning how to break away from her haunting pain. I wanted to be the first and last man to remove her from her world of loss. I wanted to create a paradise for the both of us to grow in.

"Baby, so do you. Can you hardly wait for the sound of little tiny feet?" she said, tears filling her eyes. "I can't."

Missy wanted a kid badly. In her eyes it would be the ultimate test of our union, validifying our love. But the facts of our life were loud and clear, there would be financial, mental and emotional burdens involved. It made me squirm and filled my imagination with a new level of frustration, fear and what-if's.

"We have lots still to consider, Missy, don't you think?" I asked, trying to ease into our conversation the possibility of failure. I needed to take the role of practicality, I thought.

"We have nothing against us but time, Tony, and our baby will help make time feel better," she said. "Everything else is secondary in comparison to what we can't get back, our time."

I gave in, admitting she could be right. She would help figure out our direction when the time was right, I thought, calming myself to accept what was at hand, wanting to appreciate and cherish our moment of bliss, wanting to keep her happy and protect her heart.

We navigated our way through the traffic along the Dan Ryan heading toward the Stevenson. Thoughts of baby names filled my head. Just maybe I have found the key, I thought speeding along headed home.

We continued those long weekly morning drives to Chicago from Next-to-Nowhere Illinois in March, driving to see a specialist who would be monitoring my wife for the next 3 months. We had science protecting our little bundle of love, masquerading as a joyous moment in our life together as one.

I was working 3rd shift hours, 9:00pm to 6:00am and hitting the road with my wife at 6:30am to be at the doctor's in Chicago by 9:30am.

I felt manic.

Just to please…just to show…just because…I thought to myself on a regular basis, as we drove past pastures of grazing cattle being baptized by the rays of bursting sun coming over the horizon. I always took it as a sign symbolizing love always found a way, even through beings that seemingly didn't know the validity of existing…like cattle on a hill.

All I wanted to do was break the cycle of hurt that we both were born in.

I became depressive.

Suddenly, the rains began to fall. At first slow causing the beginning of bickering, awakening us to our still existing state of unhappiness. Then it began to pour.

While trying to build a family, our marriage seemed to become more and more irrelevant, conflict took the place of joy, and we seemed less and less able to communicate.

I began studying meditation practices, trying to combat the stress, hoping to anchor us down in the sands of stability, looking to gather some form of spirituality from our state of confusion.

But the pull on sobriety for us was too strong as one problem after another surfaced, beating against our desires, the little known structure we had remaining in our life together as one. It soon became overpoweringly obvious we couldn't resolve conflict as husband and wife.

Instead, we were causing more issues.

We just couldn't see…and I began losing it.

"Hey, Missy, what do you think about this book? It lists every day of your pregnancy with different tips on how to handle your body and mind during this time," I asked her one day while browsing through a bookstore's mounds of information concerning pregnancy care for mom, baby, dad and everyone in between.

"Tony, I already have a baby book in mind, no help needed in that area," she said with a little irritation in her voice. "Where I need help is in finding out what I am going to name my baby."

"Ah, excuse me," I said unable to control my mouth. "What am I, chopped liver? Last time I checked, I was a part of this parenting thing too," I responded rather smartly, trying to keep some element of humor in the conversation.

"Tony, please, I am the one carrying this child and I should be the one who ultimately gets to make the final decision on names, books or whatever," she barked at me.

"You plan on having this baby on your own or something?" I asked, getting furious.

"You said it, not me. I'm getting tired of playing the game, so I'm not anymore."

"What are you talking about? We decided to have this child, and now this?" I responded.

She said nothing.

We walked out of the bookstore, knowing our marriage was really no more. We were going through the motions as if repetition would make change.

"Damn, Missy, just once I would like to see us be at least excited together about this. It shouldn't be so business-like. I mean we're trying to be parents again. I know you're a little scared, but we're in this together, so let's stand together in this, too, okay?" I said to her after a brutal day of waiting, testing, talking, waiting and talking again, in the doctor's office.

She said nothing, just sat staring out the window as if she was alone on a train steaming through the flatlands of Illinois.

I guess the passion that Missy and I shared about revamping our lives became a shot of magic. We were pregnant with twins. Unfortunately, almost as quickly as we discovered our miracle, two became one.

"Leaving one sounding good and looking strong in there, Mom, Dr. Bernard said rubbing Missy's hand as she laid on her back, and then turning and patting me on the shoulder. He candidly pointed out his discovery on the sono-gram humming with life in front of us. Tears had begun falling from Missy's eyes at the sight and sound of our little one's beauty dancing on the screen within his sack of pro-tection. Simultaneously, feelings of emptiness and the void of darkness attached themselves to our moment of glee.

"Missy, are you okay?" I asked, concerned.

"Just fine," she replied, unmoved by my presence or my words.

I didn't know what to say or do.

I wanted to give her the run-down about me being there for her, the run-down on how we could make it through, the run-down on how this was our second chance for not only a baby but for our marriage as well. I felt like I had done this time and time before and was allowing my words to resound off a plexi-glass dome….

So, I tried to handle it like a man.

I begin working like a Hebrew slave, to make amends for my inability to heal her wounds. I dedicated my life to trying to give her everything she wanted…and more if my body would only cooperate with my mind.

I brought her home flowers I saw on the edge of the road on my way home from work, with the fresh falling dew still clinging to its petals.

I made it a point to run bathwater and mas-sage her swelling feet since I knew her body was no longer her own.

I told her I loved her as much as I could, whenever I could, because I did.

But I kept hitting that damn wall. Scorn.

It was almost as if the button had been hit on this woman. She became as vindictive as she could possibly be, and I found myself in the middle of a whirlwind of heartache, despair and disdain. I could feel the surge of wanting to escape engulf the both of us in a grip of terror, with neither one of us wanting to let go. I felt the pain of both of our losses being magnified a billion times over, as if an elephant had sat upon my chest, breaking me down.

I wanted to run.

I was a broken vessel.

I began to take the practice of meditation seriously focusing all the energy I could muster, towards trying to be for my wife, becoming a protection for her health and for our bundle of love. I couldn't imagine any other woman I would rather have bring our child into the world. No matter what the cause.

I knew between us, our child wouldn't only be loved passionately, but create a shared love as well. He would stand the test of time. He stood above all of the worldly cries, trumping reality.

I felt as if I was flying on the pure wings of love, certainly out of step with reality. I wanted nothing more than to be for Missy, willing to rearrange my beliefs and behavior for her. I was willing to do anything to keep her mine.

During a phone conversation with Bobby one Saturday evening before I had to be at work, I laid bare the essence of my relationships. Bobby had become a distant Tony-fixer-upper during my second marriage. I was hoping to stop the fall of Missy and I, and I looked for help from wherever I could afford to reveal the weaknesses hiding within my character.

Eventually after feeling Bobby's head full of my misery, he told me about his upcoming wedding to his college sweetheart.

"Tony, Tony," I heard Missy say with a poke from behind me, starling me a bit since I had left her sleeping in the bedroom only a few minutes ago.

"Hold on for a second, B," I said turning towards Missy. "Yeah, wassup," I said, realizing I was irritated and showing it after the words had began to form.

"Let me speak to Bobby."

"Why?"

"Just give me the phone," she said reaching forward and snatching it from my hand.

"Hey Bobby, how are you? Missy said with a completely different tone of voice and a high-beam headlight type of glare at me as she walked away with the phone toward the kitchen, settling against the countertop. She returned back to her conversation, which became a confession of sort.

"Congratulation on your engagement. I bet she is so happy. She's got herself a good man, make sure you tell her that. I wish I would've found someone like you. How lucky she must feel?" she said, batting her eyes toward me, as I looked on in shock and awe. This woman hadn't shown even the affection of a hello, a how was my sleep greeting, and here she was pouring on an emotional bath of wonderment, desire and passion to Bobby.

She unceremoniously strolled across the room, glancing past me out the bay window at the view overlooking hole number nine of a well-manicured public course.

"I really wish you were more like Bobby," she said matter-of-factly. "I mean, he comes

from a great family; he's very nice and loving
and he's easy to talk to…if only," she trailed
off.

I just looked at her.

I couldn't even form words.

I was literally shocked to tears.

"You're a bitch," I finally managed to mumble, "and I hate the day I ever met you."

I walked out the door, shaking my head in
disgust, feeling my insides twist, smelling the
smoke from my mind burning an imprint of those
words on every neuron. I sat on a park bench
over looking the par 3 18th, thinking, recalcu-
lating.

My best friend was one of the closest
people to me in the world, and she knew this
and went there anyway, I thought.

"Such malice and scorn. What have I done?"
I whispered, hearing a scream.

"FORE!"

I ducked, throwing my hands up, bracing for
the point of impact. A little extra-added pain
never hurt anyone, I thought, especially me.

None came.

I looked up and saw three guys walking toward me, lugging their golf bags behind them on
pull carts. They were excited and giving each
other high fives. I walked toward the hole
looking for the ball, to let them know the
spot. As I got closer to the hole I saw a hole
in one.

"You must survive and you will stay alive,"
I heard a gruff voice from above my head say as
I lay in my hospital bed in a daze of confusion
with a deep unknown longing nagging at my flut-
tering will.

I opened my eyes to find my grandfather staring down at me with his deep, dark, heavy brown eyes, covered by a pair of wild brows with hairs that seemed to dance every which way. He had been a US Marine who lived by the credo once a Marine, always a Marine. He had a mysterious glow of power and belief. He had been dead four years, but came to me on that day, the day I was letting go of reality, looking to fly to another world far away from the pain of trying to be loved.

"Dying is not an option," he said. "There is work still left to be done, and I'll be damned if you're going home without finishing your chores," he said, as if I had been tasked to clean up the yard of pine needles that had fallen from the swaying trees.

"Yes, granddad," I offered up weakly, unable to fathom the difference between reality and void.

I felt my grandmother put her hand on my forehead.

"Are you alright, baby?" she asked, looking exhausted as I peered at her through half-closed eyes.

"Fine…tell granddad I'm fine," I said.

"Okay, baby, get some more rest," she said, pulling the covers up to my neck, tucking me deeper into my bed of illusion. "Your face is burning up, we gotta sweat that fever out of you still.

I drifted away

After that night Missy and I became total lunatics toward one another. We made something that was supposed to be so beautiful, so new, so healing, so eventful and so miraculous dark, dingy and damaged.

I felt crushed, again and again as the questions began to resurface.

How could you? Why would you? Why even try? What about the baby? What about Missy (still)? What about you (now)? my mind exclaimed to me every moment. I couldn't do anything without questions. My spirit felt empty and depleted, my mind overwhelmed, my heart filled with noise that kept pouring in.

We were trapped, I thought, and I am to blame. I needed a way, a path, but first, I had to face my fears, the what if's, how come's and the why's.

So, we made an answer appear, but not without a little help.

I moved out of the house the first time when she was about four months pregnant. We couldn't see eye-to-eye on anything.

I was working too much; I wasn't working enough.

I was unkind; I was too kind.

I was insensitive; I was too sensitive.

I was not like my best friend whom she wished she had met instead of me; I was everything she ever wanted and more.

She hated me; she loved me.

She was leaving me as soon as the baby was born; she was planning on us having more children.

She hated the sight of me; she wanted me around forever.

On and on and on we went, back and forth, up and down.

I rationalized it all.

I realized it all.

I knew she was pregnant and had heard how it would be.

I tried to remain true, but it just didn't seem right, I told myself time and time again.

My new mentor Mr. D and his wife took me in, refusing to allow me to spend money seeking a place of refuge on my own. During my stay, I began speaking to and taking notes from Mr. D, crying to him again about Missy and the "deranged state of living now playing out in the lives of Tony and Missy Part II," and he began chuckling, just like my dad had done years before.

He said, "Young man, young man, I told you that playing with fire will get you burned. What did you think was going to happen after you let your past become your present? Did you think you was gonna have a cakewalk of a future? Shucks, you might as well hang on and enjoy the ride 'cause it's only gonna get more and more erratic now. This ain't nothing but the beginning, junior," he said, leaning back in his chair like an ol' judge passing down a verdict.

My shoulders dropped, and I felt the tears begin to fall down my face as I stared out into the darkness inside the jail.

David reached over across the table and handed me a wad of white toilet paper, hard as cardboard.

"It ain't Charmin, junior, but go ahead, wipe your face," he said. "You're a good man, but you're a little twisted about love, confusing it with them books and movies you young people like to get into. Did you forget the hero always dies or gets busted up trying to rescue the damn damsel? Even if you didn't, which I know you didn't, have you ever heard of something called woman's intuition?"

I nodded my head yes in response.

"Never believed in it much before did ya?"

I shook my head no.

"Stay strong, little brother, stay strong," he said, disappearing through the dark catwalk connecting our two pods.

I felt defeated and trapped, a feeling I had once upon a time vowed I would never feel again.

After having moved in and out of the house several times throughout the course of Missy's pregnancy, I managed to convince Missy into letting me be present for the birth.

Throughout this exchange of home again, out again, I received a revelation from god, like Jake in the Blues Brothers, to go back, once and for all, for better or worse.

Manic.

So, I did, with the first item on my agenda of righting a wrong. I had to sit Missy down and reveal my infidelity, listing my reasons why, confessing my wrong.

I could see Mr. D in my thoughts, shaking his head saying, "Be strong, young brother, be strong."

But, I soon discovered again what I already knew, Missy and I could never resolve anything.

In fact most of our resolutions began new issues on top of the unresolved old ones.

"Missy, this is crap! How you gonna be mad over nothing?" I screamed from the kitchen into the bedroom at her.

She was upset over an old phone bill with Cynthia's number appearing on it from calls I had made with my calling card linked to our home line.

"You know I solved that months ago," I said.

"I've been trying to make things right with you, woman. It's you I want! But for what? Look at you now! You're acting as if you couldn't care less, like I would fuck around on you after giving you the best that I got!" I said, motioning toward the living room where Michael was resting in his playpen.

"You're being silly and acting like an insane bitch and you're not seeing me!" I yelled, feeling exhausted and lightheaded.

I walked toward the living room with my head hung low from having emptied myself, again.

I turned, looking over my shoulder, barely able to catch a glimpse of Missy running toward me swinging wildly.

I ducked and picked her up, pinning her on the sofa, as Michael began stirring, awakening to the screams of his mother, and the shouts of his father.

"Missy, what the hell you think you're doing? You can't whoop my ass, so you might as well stop pretending!" I said, letting her go.

I got up and walked towards the kitchen to get a drink of water.

I heard her screaming, and turned…

A crystal angel, how beautiful.

"CRACK! CRACK!"

The sadistic sound of beauty went right upside my head, twice.

I was floating, succumbing, falling on my knees as if in prayer, seeing stars, bleeding love, feeling eternal.

I could hear my son screaming bloody murder with heavy sobs, and could feel drops of warm, rain-like tears falling from Missy's eyes.

"I'm sorry, Tony, I'm sorry! Let me get a towel," she said, stumbling over her words. "Oh my god, what have I done? What have I done? I'm so sorry. I'm so sorry. I've got to call 911."

"No, don't, I'm fine," I said in a low tone, trying to keep her from involving a third party, knowing what would happen.

Missy continued to freak out, finally deciding to call an ambulance, when the blood shooting from my head soaked one towel, and began seeping through a second. I got it together enough to calm her, encouraging her to breathe, slow down and focus on quieting Michael. He had been screaming for 20 minutes as if he felt our pain. He had witnessed someone he loved go down in a heap of swelteringly purified flames.

Buddhists have it right. It's amazing how Rigpa can be achieved during some of the most obvious, but missed moments of time. All things in life I had felt mattered most didn't matter at all as long as I kept trying to control the way they looked, felt and must be. In that moment of time, I learned to let go and embrace the totality of my nature and current life situation. I felt as though I had learned to fly without the need for wings.

Too bad I had to experience it with my head cracked open; it could have been more enjoyable otherwise, and more lasting.

I began coaching Missy on how we would describe what had taken place between us as an accident during play.

"I was just teaching you how to defend yourself, okay?" I reasoned, not realizing the severity of it all.

She said nothing.

We would get through it, I tried to reassure her, still on my knees, unable to justify moving from my newfound, stable state of being.

She didn't listen.

She told the very first emergency personnel on the scene exactly what she had done.

It was as though she was trying to exercise the demons from our world by sacrificing herself.

I was hurt.

Lying on the stretcher, looking between the arms of one of the paramedics, seeing the cops putting the cuffs on my wife, listening to Michael's song of pain, I wanted nothing more than to fly away with Missy and Michael under my wings.

I lifted my head, trying to scream as they rolled me out of our apartment, but I blacked out.

I still wanted nothing more than to start anew with Missy.

I wanted nothing more than to be there for her, to be her friend, confidant, to husband myself in the pureness of her shame.

I wanted to become her love.

***********Memphite Feathering***********

Open Up Your Eye

Keep being a lily among roses
Revealing the delicateness of your beauty
Dashing in nature, splendid and warm
Keep daring to tempt Nature into being your friend
Standing tall against the wind...
Moving right along –
Lovingly painting yourself before the setting Sun
Knowing very well through listening change becomes
Keep running as if time is of the essence,
Of pure joy, of unexplainable nothingness,
Of trite restraint.
Keep it to yourself never what is of you
For it is in doing when perhaps you find you –
Swimming in a sea of collective thoughts,
Pools of sounds, mounds of energy free
Wondering will she ever see?

TL

***********Memphite Feathering***********

I convinced Missy that we needed to try again, trying desperately to lift us up. With every atom in my body harmonized, I focused my energy exclusively on helping to heal our dying paradise, the place in which we wanted our family to prosper, growing the place we called home.

We went to marriage counseling and learned techniques to improve communication, which only made us smarter, allowing us to readily identify each other's flaws. We began strategizing carefully against one another, trying to avoiding becoming victims, again.

It was amazing how easily we could point out each other's weaknesses.

Our newfound attention to detail would have been a good thing if we were more open minded and loving in the process, but we didn't know how to be, and because of the gap in knowing the true nature of ourselves, our love for one another broke down every time light-years before we even knew why.

We continued to dance, with no room to breathe, moving, spinning toward our destruction.

I began to take notice of the way in which life was allowing me to have some say into creating my masterpiece. I hadn't noticed before, always striving to be pleasing, to be wanted, to be a conqueror, to be loved.

Once again I wanted to make things work and they had not, for all involved, yet time ticked on and the rest is history… ancient history it seems sometimes, but not all the time, like now…

Perpetual Growth

In times of darkness, life can seem so bleak
In times of darkness, answers are meek
In times of darkness, all valleys are low
In times of darkness, there seems no room to grow
In times of darkness, pain equals atomic size
In times of darkness, there is no place to hide
In times of darkness, morning never seems to come
In times of darkness, we must run on
Then, the day breaks and we see so clear
In times of darkness, there's no need to fear
In times of darkness, life is surreal
In times of darkness, peace is revealed
In times of darkness, all answers flow through being
In times of darkness, there are no stings
In times of darkness, valleys are places of rest
In times of darkness, we all are blessed
In times of darkness, space abounds galore
In times of darkness, the Earth shows her splendor
more than before
In times of darkness, weakness escapes through pain
In times of darkness, no need to refrain
In times of darkness, morning is intensified by dark
In times of darkness, follow your heart
In times of darkness, essence is truly revealed
In times of darkness, you are healed...

TL

Once a dream, now a catastrophe, I thought as I sat reading The Tibetan Book of Living and Dying, trying to make heads and tails of my new dilemmas.

I had always pictured myself as a doer, an accomplisher, a dreamer, and a reality maker. Now, I found myself on the verge of destroying an innocent spirit's chance at the balance of a family. I loved Michael more than I did anything up to that moment.

But, there I was, unable to properly love and honor his mother, I thought, reading about the wickedness of humankinds endless search for individual wants and desires, samsara.

I didn't want to hurt, but I had no clue how to let go, so I read.

After our son Michael was born, I took some time off from work to help Missy get settled in having to take care of a newborn. It was one of the few free flowing times of our marriage, seemingly bonding us a little more, helping us let go of some of our past issues.

"Missy, I've been thinking of maybe finding a new job that will give us more time together. What do you think?" I asked her one evening after dinner, while listening to Miles Davis blow his horn.

Michael was taking one of the 15 naps he took on a daily (lucky munchkin).

"Well, Tony, we had planned to both be in school within a year or so of moving here, plus you have the veteran's affairs services, so I say go for it. I sure could use the help," she said softly, as if our conversation was something she had been wishing and wanting to have, too.

I began to think that our marriage could work.

She was thinking sensibly.

I presented something to her calmly and we came to a consensus rather easily, even after the violence of a few weeks before.

Wow, just maybe, I thought.

"Okay, financially it will be tough for a while, but we'll get by. I will begin looking, get myself registered for school, and we can figure out a schedule for lil' man that works for both of us. How's that?" I asked.

We were trying for the first time since we had gotten to Illinois.

"I think it sounds like a plan."

"I love you Missy, through thick and thin," I said to her with a gleam in my eye, because I did.

"I know, and I love you, too," she said as we leaned toward one another sharing a passionate kiss resembling the one we shared when we said I do.

By the time I found a suitable job, my severance pay from my time spent as a corrections officer dwindled to nothing, and my wife's love and patience had combusted. We were once again exhibiting hate toward one another with such force it was hard to maintain any semblance of balance.

And my being a non-traditional student at Bradley University, studying Communications and Philosophy, made matters worse. She had begun hating me for taking our words and putting them into action, forming our reality.

I again began to feel alone.

Finances ruled.

I moved out again, running toward the only place that had provided me with stability, myself.

I needed to find some peaceful resolution to our state of anger.

I had to remain and show love, affection and attention to Michael.

Fighting against the impossibility of concentration, never quite grasping the force of living in turmoil with love.

Depressive.

I got through The Tibetan Book of Living and Dying feeling as though I had indeed tripped up the rabbit hole toward the unknown, learning to be okay, immediately beginning to read the Tao Te Ching, noticing the subtle similarities to The Word, trying to hear my grandmother's words, but hearing nothing.

I wanted to make it all right.

I had to.

It was my duty.

I had to find peace for us all, even if it killed me, I told myself one evening after leaving my logic class.

But, I knew I wasn't making logical sense.

As I drove toward Missy, the sway of the trees casting shadows along the road seemed to agree with me.

So, I continued.

"Missy, I know it has been rough for us, but we vowed for better or worse. I want to try to make things right. We did this for life, you know?" I said below Missy's bedroom window as she looked down at me.

"Tony, I do love you, but we've been through hell. Do you really think we can make

it through this and have a strong future together?"

"I don't know, but I want to try," I said.

"I'm scared."

"Baby we can do this," I begged. I had everything I needed to make it right, I just had
to find a way.

"We'll see. Goodnight, Tony," she said,
closing the window and disappearing behind the
sky blue curtains pulled shut behind her.

I looked down at myself, at my green pul-
lover shirt with black sweatpants, and brown
slip-on shoes, with a worn Carolina Tarheel cap
tucked down over my face. I realized I wouldn't
give myself a chance either, looking the way I
looked that night.

We were on hold, waiting to see if we would
begin trying to make love happen between us
again. I began to meditate more, making it the
center of all my actions, wanting nothing more
than to be the protector of my sacred love - my
family.

I had moved into my own place, a dump of a
building that was once a motel. It had brown
shaggy old carpet filled with the smell of
mildew, and it was the place of choice for
prostitutes, druggies and all other types of
people down on their luck. My room overlooked a
parking lot with constant nightly performances,
from dramas demonstrating the perils of human-
kind to the occasional cops show, invariably
ending with someone's blood being spilled
across the ground. I observed all of this
through dirt-colored sheers that use to be
white from a bed that sprung up and down like a
trampoline.

I was alone and isolated.

I had no family or friends to turn to near
by.

I began feeling the signs of abandonment entering all around me, as if in payment for past lives lived, a feeling I last felt as a young boy watching and feeling my mother's rejection over and over again as men entered and exited her life.

I felt strapped into a ride that seemed to bring joy and sheer pleasure to others, but which caused only pure pain and resentment to myself.

Lao Tzu's, the great founder of Taoism, words, "if you find your roots and nourish them, you will know longevity. If you live a long creative life, you will leave a legacy," calmed my aching spirit, but left my heart longing all the more.

I realized the scars of my life had yet to heal, and I became engrossed in knowing why they had not and wondering if they ever would.

School became a catalyst of discovery for me, causing me to wonder out loud, pondering the certainty of everything.

I wasn't fully aware of it, but I began to change my perception of the world. By not just merely being a part of it, but by becoming an observer of what went into it, from my actions of choice, to the influence of those whom I shared my life with, I became aware.

And sure enough, on track with my new dis-covery came a growth in pain from my reality. Many developments and twists of fate had oc-curred in the saga of love between Missy and me, ushering in others besides just her and I.

I decided to try even more.

Michael was the direct recipient of our re-lations with one another, and because of him I began feeling as though I could not know enough about life and the many levels of existing among people, animals, and all other forces of living.

I became engrossed in the how all things communicated beyond verbal language, and beyond noticeable acts.

I began to see the energy of life.

Since I had done so badly with my own relationships, I wanted to know why and what life and love had in common.

Missy wanted things to be the same as they were when we first met and didn't adjust to the new me.

I saw things differently and wanted to push us toward newer ways of being, thinking and doing.

I wanted to see the world and explore it together, looking at all things and people as a different us, manifesting love.

She didn't understand.

The problem became more obvious as we began spending more time with one another, looking for possibilities around the fringe of impossible.

Still, we tried, deciding again to merge our homes, both wanting the true meaning of home to resonate as being the reason why we lived.

We both thought it best we try for the sake of Michael having both of his parents equally giving him time and love.

Instead, we began to argue...again.

"Tony, who are you? I mean I don't get where all this is coming from. All of a sudden, just because you've been going to school, you think you're better than somebody now?" Missy asked me one morning as I was getting ready for school.

She and Michael had been spending time at my place, testing the water, and she had decided to stay the night there so we could be together before I went to school and work the next day.

I didn't really have time to get into an argument with her. I still had to warm-up my old boat of a car, get my books packed, get out the door by 8:45, find parking, which would take at least 20 minutes, and get to class before 9:30. I knew if I said the wrong thing, I would be fighting with her until 10:30. And, I was tired from not getting much sleep after staying awake most of the night, listening for any cause for alarm while Michael and Missy slept.

"Missy, I am just trying not to be so close-minded," I said calmly as I walked out of the bedroom to grab my coat and the keys to the car.

She came behind me, and I could feel the energy of her agitation and disgust envelop me, enticing me to tangle with her.

"What are you saying, Mr. Tony, that all the rest of us po' folks are ignorant and stupid just because we believe in tradition?" she snapped.

"Did I say that, Missy? Why you always try to put words in my mouth, woman?" I asked with a little agitation of my own.

I tried to show my wife my desire to elevate above class, stereotypes, dogmatism, mediocre perception, etc, etc.

None of which she bought.

And I missed my class.

She grabbed Michael, who had been jarred from his sleep, bundled him up and promptly marched out of my dingy room as if I was an epidemic to run from and avoid.

The look in Michael's eyes spoke volumes. He was perplexed, shocked, peaceful, sad, happy and angry, all at once...exactly my point of view.

After they left, I decided to go for a drive through the countryside of Central Illinois, trying to get away from the developing devastation of yet another crumbling moment in our life.

I couldn't see why it had come to this again, but as the dead leaves of Fall tumbled down along the winding back roads, I began studying how all of the collective moments of our life together came to be.

I tried desperately to see.

As I drove deeper and deeper into the countryside, cows wandered along every hillside, and the houses looked as if they could sleep ten or more people comfortably, it occurred to me how I had become accustomed to being a superman of sorts. I always tried to take women away from their miseries, in spite of my own wants and desires. I felt it was my duty to do so because I had always wished someone, anyone, would have done so for my mother.

"Lord, I'm in trouble, won't you lead me?" I heard my mom singing one day while cleaning dishes in our three-bedroom project house, standing among the hundreds of other similar houses cut out in the red-clay of southern Georgia.

"Ma, why are you in trouble?" I asked her, half expecting to get slapped and told to stay in my place, half eager to know if there was something I could do to help.

She looked at me and began to cry. I held her and we cried together. I knew what she felt and knew about her burdens being too heavy to hold on her own and too heavy to share with her child.

Later that week, I took some of that burden anyway, finding a job working as a stock-boy to bring in any money I could to help my family survive.

I was nine...

As I drove along, with tears running down my face, I began to fade in with my surroundings, and I could see why Sam, Cynthia and Missy loved me but didn't want to travel for life with me. I could carry a load, but it was always a bumpy-ride. Smooth sailing was only a made-up dream I used to conquer their love. Once on board, they all seemed to sense my trickery and fought to abandon ship.

Now I have a son, what do I do? I asked myself as I pulled over, unaware of the sprinkles of rain beginning to fall, coinciding with the wetness of forgotten tears falling down my face.

I parked under a giant oak tree still holding on to its leaves of yellows, oranges, reds and browns. My spot faced out over a field of nothingness for miles. I sat and stared as the rain began to fall harder and the beating of my heart seemed to grow fainter.

I was determined to will something good from the depths of that barren field.

My mind raced back and forth, projecting images of my childhood problems alongside my new adult ones. They seemed to match, as if I was playing Old Maid.

My mother yelling at me for my lack of understanding, my wife crying because of my yelling for lack of understanding; visions of me walking along the streets as a child looking to do any dead-end or odd job to make money, being a married man without a job that paid all our bills...

Where does it all end? I thought as I drove off, heading back into town, not sure where home was.

Time seemed to have drifted away, beckoning night with all of its considerable darkness.

***********Tipping Point***********

Remembrance

Do this while keeping in mind,
Walk softly but disturb much,
Question everything, while having a solemn view,
Entangle oneself into something meaningful,
Focus beyond your individual desires
Do all of this in style, with purpose, with grace

Open up to the world around,
Center oneself while staying true,
Laugh soundly but stay reserved,
Speak with joy and great contemplation,
Know that great moments come from great expectations
- spawned by even greater patience
Open doors beyond despair.

Place oneself on a grounding that's true,
Grasp for nothing and remain at ease,
Listen with patience that stops time,
Encourage growth through testing ways,
Firmly rooted with clarity in hand
Live life in perspective again.

Love all things in all and all
Remember from beginning to end
Hold together and balance with an infinite touch
Summon energy from worlds unknown but felt
Tenderly emphasize peace
Love from greatest to least…

TL

***********Tipping Point***********

I worked daily before and after school, helping with the counseling needs of veterans who had disabilities, setbacks and pain, and it was here I met some very influential people who would help steer the course of change in my life. I wanted to make my family work and was miserable because it had not, and everyone saw it and could feel it from the moment I walked through the door.

"What's up, Tony? How you feeling this morning? You look like death warmed over," asked William one of the other student-aides, as soon as I walked through the door after a long weekend of absent thoughts, tormented feelings and hopeless mending with Missy.

"Ummm hmmm," I mumbled, "I'm doing okay. Definitely have seen better days."

"Tony, you have to let it go, man, before you get yourself in a world of hurt."

I had heard him say this many times before.

"It always works itself out; stop forcing it, dude," he said while patting me on the back as I sat down. "Besides, we got work to do, no need for you to bring that shit in here anyway."

"Will," I said, facing the short guy with the military-style high and tight haircut, brain of a forensic scientist and heart of a lion. He had endured twenty-plus years of military service, as well as a broken marriage himself, "I want this."

"I know you do, but you don't need it. This doesn't define you. I know you think it does because of your son and your pride, but trust me, man, all it's going to bring you is more pain than you can handle. A scorned woman in the past is still a scorned woman."

"I hear ya, man. I gotta get to work before I have to get out of here. Do you need a ride to school today?" I asked. We both attended Bradley, Will for education, and me, it seemed, for clarity.

"Yeah, that's cool. Think about what I'm saying to you, Tony. Don't be a fool, man," he said.

I nodded my head up and down, trying to assure him and myself that I got his message loud and clear. I heard him, but something just wasn't clicking. I knew something wasn't adding up.

How was it possible I still felt empty and incomplete? I asked myself on the way to school that day with Will jamming to Pink Floyd, unaware of my dismantling.

I kept asking this question over and over again as I played with my son, as I helped out on a group project for school that required my full participation and attention, which I couldn't give, even as I sat in a coffee shop trying to relax by watching the traffic hurry along. I kept feeling the throb of the unknown beating its way into the known.

Thoughts of my failure in love crept into everything I touched.

They hunted me.

I knew there had to be more to my story, and I was determined to find the end, I rationalized, forgetting the wisdom of Eastern perils and accounts of true Western reasoning I had spent so much time studying.

My unbalanced emotions led me around by my nose.

In the world of physical reality, Missy decided to remain apart from me and see other people. She needed to have fun in her life since the last four years had been a living hell. She told me I hadn't been much fun.

Her fun people were of the sort we had vowed we would never bring around Michael, people who couldn't care less about overall child development, just plain self-full-feel-me.

I became enraged, demanding Missy reassess the company she kept, one day after picking up my son for an afternoon in the park.

"Missy, I am not feeling good about these new-found friends of yours being so involved in Michael's life. I mean, you know I know what they're all about since I used to lock up their asses. Come on now, what about what we said we wouldn't do, that doesn't matter anymore?" I asked, feeling my stomach turn on the inside. I had just opened a can of worms and I was no longer sure I wanted to bait and fish any further.

"First of all, you need to keep your nose out of my business. And second, who are you? What are you doing? Do you think that I am going to sit back and watch you move on with your sorry-ass life while I sit around crying about it and not move on with my own? Hell NO!" she said, throwing her whole body into every word as if she had been dying to explode with this newly found freedom.

I only wanted to tell her she needed to watch what and whom she brought around our son and to watch herself with the kind of men she was entertaining, but it didn't come out like I was helping or wanting to help. It only moved her to defense and anger.

"Look, Missy, all I am saying is you just need to watch yourself, that's all…"

"Naw, you better watch yourself!" she snapped. "They might end up killing your ass," she said, turning and walking toward her car, never looking back as she got in and speeding away.

I'll be damned, I thought. I was stunned.

Where was this coming from? I asked myself, too choked up to play with Michael as he went up and down the slide, oblivious to our fury. I couldn't even respond back to her in my mind. There were no words, visions or chemicals producing feelings of any kind. I hadn't known we were to a point of elimination.

I was numb.

I became even more defensive and paranoid about my son's safety, beginning to try and catch up with her daily, but I could never find her at home.

I became frantic.

I decided I would campout in my boat-mobile outside of her house, waiting to talk.

I had been receiving stupid threats from disguised voices and 1-8-7 (a code for murder of cops) text messages in my phone.

I went outside of boundaries I had always believed in, calling her mother, brother, sister and her friends, trying to track her down to make this issue go away.

I was determined to force peace from our hell by any means necessary.

I knew I needed to confront her about the threat.

I also knew it could easily become very real.

I waited.

Finally, she showed up with Michael asleep in his car seat. It was after 10:00 pm.

I let it rip right there in the parking lot before she even got out of the car. It was all or nothing.

And it was, in my mind.

"What the fuck do you think you're doing! Look, Missy, all this shit is stupid. What the hell is this open-ended threatening crap? I thought we were much bigger than that! I would never do anything to hurt or harm you intentionally, directly or indirectly, so why the fuck not the same from you? Huh? Fucking answer me! Why not?" I asked, feeling the lump in my throat growing bigger with every word that fell from my lips.

"Boy, what are you talking about? Why you all emotional and out of control now? Because I have moved on?" she smirked.

"Missy, it has nothing to do with that at all," I said, getting my composure and realizing we were still in the parking lot of her apartment complex. "I understand you've moved on, my only concern is for the safety of Michael and, of course, of you too, but it doesn't make any damn sense that your new friends would feel the need to send me threats. What if they decide to act on them and Michael happens to be with me at the time, then what? Have you thought of that?" I asked. "I'm not trying to control you or even tell you what to do with your life. I'm just asking you to think about it," I finished, pulling Michael from his car seat.

We walked upstairs toward her apartment, and a crazy thing happened. She actually agreed with me and called her friends, telling them it was over, explaining she needed time to herself to get things in order.

"I didn't mean for you to end your relationships, Missy. I was simply..."

"I didn't do that for you, Tony. I did it for Michael and me. I know when I'm wrong, and I don't have a problem correcting my mistakes no matter how much I may stand to lose," she said as she walked into the bathroom, closing the door behind her.

"Missy, we both made mistakes and sometimes seeing through them allows you to see what's right and what's wrong, what's good and what's bad," I said to her through the bathroom door. "I think this is good."

"What's this?" she asked, cracking the bathroom door, peaking out and revealing a face wet with tears.

"Our family," I said pushing the bathroom door open and passionately embracing her in my arms as if I was holding her for the first time.

"Are you sure?"

"Definitely." I said, cutting her off, not wanting to hear anything else. I saw an opening again, and I took it.

And like that, we were back to living together, again, believing something new was on the horizon...something promising and true...something undefined.

For several weeks it seemed we could do no wrong, and our love for one another shined. We tried hard to acknowledge the significance of each other and the magnitude of yet another new beginning, fighting against the reality of the emptiness filling our history.

Soon it became increasingly more evident we were not meant to be.

"What are we doing? I mean, Tony, you and I are like old people. I work and you study and we watch Michael grow. I need more!" she yelled at me one day.

I was trying. I wanted to love her with actions that made words, with renewed views, without overused metaphors and clichés of passion and desire.

I was willing myself against being fake wanting to penetrate the barriers of all those yesterday's news and tomorrow's preconceived blues.

I thought I was loving her with no drama.

"Missy, baby, I know we can do this, we just have to…"

"I don't want to do this! You're boring, uncaring and insensitive. You just wanted me back here so you could be closer to Michael. I might as well just be a piece of furniture to you, just taking up space…"

"Missy, that's not true, I love you. What do you want from me?"

"Nothing."

"Okay," I said, grabbing my book bag, walking out the door.

I went to school in shambles, knowing I couldn't afford to miss any more days since I had already managed to slither my way into excused absences from several professors for missed time. No more excuses would do.

I came back home later in the evening to see her packing her things, preparing to move back into her recently abandoned place.

I walked in and gave my little man, who was crying, a hug and kiss.

He was burning up with fever.

"Missy, you need to get Michael to the doctor, he's hot as hell," I said to her.

"There you go again. Coming into the house and handing out orders, like you're the boss or something. I am sick of this shit, Tony. Do you hear me? I am fucking sick of all of this shit!" she screamed at me, throwing a pillow from the couch my way.

"You're tripping," I said. "Just get Michael to the doctor and stop acting like a dumb bitch. I don't have time for this. If you would have been paying attention to him, you wouldn't

have that type of craziness on your brain, but
you're too busy feeling sorry for yourself,
neglecting our son. What the hell?" I said,
walking down the hall toward the bedroom, feeling the disgust beginning to build within me,
realizing I was only adding shame to an already
shameful turn of events in our lives.

"Fuck you, Tony," she said, throwing a pillow toward me as I went past her.

She took Michael, leaving a bomb barrage of
malice behind.

I stood my ground, feverishly protecting
what I thought was fair territory built from a
reasonable foundation of choices we both made
time and time again.

With the slam of the front door I knew they
had returned from the doctor's office.

"How is he?" I asked from the back room
where I was stretched out on the bed studying.

I received coldness and quietness in return.

I got up and left my reading behind. I was
convinced I had some control in this situation
and I merely had to defuse the argument and
start fresh.

"Missy, did you not hear me? I was asking
how's Michael doing. Is he okay?"

"What do you care? You're just a selfish
mutherfucker who's heartless and preoccupied
with other things. But, that's okay, you're
going to get yours, you best believe."

"What are you talking about, Missy? Why are
you acting like a poor me? Why don't you just
let it go?"

"I am. Starting with you first," she said
pointing her middle finger at me.

I chuckled out loud, waving my hand in a shooing movement toward her.

"Fine. I am better off without you anyway," I let slip from my mind out of my mouth before I could catch myself.

"You ain't shit, Tony. I hate you and I hope you fucking die," she said with a look of malice. Tears were finally absent from her face.

"Likewise."

The dam broke...

Face to face we stood yelling and cursing, oblivious to our screaming baby boy.

Then it happened...

KUPLUNK!

I got knocked in the head with the television remote after getting too close.

In an instant I reacted, pushing my half-closed hand into her face, and in same instant countering to catch her before she fell, apologizing profusely.

But, the damage was done, deed performed and the reality of my bleakest moment in love set.

Her face instantaneously began to swell and her eye began to shut.

In a moment's time, I realized I had caused her considerable damage and simultaneously shattered my ego.

I had become a part of something I had fought against my whole life, never could understand and always hated...

I stumbled along, going as fast as my little legs could carry me while holding on to a suitcase full of clothes in my left hand and dragging my baseball bat in the right to defend us as we went.

Pretty soon, we saw headlights and my heart began to jump from my chest. I knew without a doubt it was the Enforcer giving chase. And he never knew how to let anything lie. I gripped my bat tighter and trudged on. We could soon hear the unmistakable sound of his copper-colored, beat-up Ford pick-up truck gaining ground behind us. We kept on going.

"Linda! Linda! God damn it woman, I know you hear me," the dark man yelled.

"What!? What could you possibly want now? What!?" my mom fired back, stopping and staring at the large man emerging from his truck.

"Don't you touch my mama!" I said to him, gripping my baseball bat tight with both hands until my fingers tingled.

"Boy, you better shut your fucking mouth and stay in your place!" he yelled.

"I don't want no goddamn babies, Linda," he screamed at my mom, "and you gotta do something about this."

"I'm not getting rid of this child, take it or leave it!" my mom screamed as tears streamed down her face and her voice began to crack.

She turned and began walking away. My sister and I followed close behind like her centurion guards. The dark man reached out and grabbed her, pulling her arm and jerking her back toward him, simultaneously bringing his free hand forward, smacking my mom in the face and down to the ground.

"You hear what I said, woman, I don't want this!" he yelled down from above her as if he was the god of pain and rejection.

I ran toward him with full force, swinging my bat wildly. I was going to kill and beat the evilness I saw in him to death.

"Eeeehhhh," I yelled, crying violently and swinging desperately for his head.

He caught the bat on the fourth swing, throwing it in the road.

WHAM. He struck me in the face with so much force I thought he had knocked my teeth down my throat, dropping me like a sack of potatoes. I went down next to my mother and heard the cries of my little sister coming from above us. Blood poured from my mouth.

"That's what you get, you little bastard. What did you think, that you could whoop me or something? You dumb ass!" he yelled, kicking me in my butt as he walked off back toward his truck.

I laid there until his truck drove off, hugging my mother, trying to console her and stop her from crying. My little sister looked on in horror and disbelief, unable to do anything but cry herself.

"Mama, you gotta leave him," I whispered into her ear.

"I know, baby," she said, sitting upright. "I know."

I wanted to call an ambulance; I wanted to take her to the hospital; I wanted to help calm Michael down, who was once again screaming, but she refused and drove herself and my baby away.

More than anything, I wanted to take it back and walk away from not only this time, but also the very first time.

More than anything, I wanted my family back.

I wept.

Then I sat and waited for the cops to come and pick me up.

As I sat on my living room floor looking
out the window at the sun beginning to set, I
rehashed what had taken place over and over in
my head, and I couldn't fight back the tears I
had held inside for what seemed like forever
and a day.

I wanted to die.

The phone rang.

I didn't want to answer but felt I should,
just in case the authorities needed to know
where to come to haul me away.

I forced myself toward the phone blaring in
the kitchen.

"Hello."

"What's up, dude, what are you doing?" the
voice on the other end asked.

"Who is this?" I asked in a slummy voice,
feeling filthier by the moment.

"What do you mean, who's this? It's Will.
What's wrong, dude? You sound like you just
lost your best friend or something."

"I just…" I began, choking up and unsure of
how to form the words of past images, "I hit my
wife, man," I cried out over the phone, "and I
don't know what I am going to do." I began,
sobbing uncontrollably, unconcerned about what
Will thought of me.

"Dude, I will be right there," he said,
hanging up quickly.

I sat listening to the silence come through
the line of the phone, white noise that seemed
to tease the disparity of my moment.

I threw it out of my hand, watching it slam
against the refrigerator, shattering into un-
equal pieces, as if mocking my life.

I curled up in a tight ball on the floor
beside the pieces of the shattered phone and
cried.

It was hands-down the worst day of my life.

Will came walking through the door, un-locked and partially open from Missy's exit. He found me lying there in the darkening apart-ment.

"What happened, Tony?"

I tried to remember the catastrophic events as best as I could. I recounted them as Will stood breathing in the stale poison of his Marlboro cigarettes above me, filling me with more gaseous vapors of death, as if I needed help in dying.

"Well," said Will calmly, "there ain't no sense in you lying here on the floor crying about it and feeling sorry for yourself. I told you this was going to happen, but you have to live and learn on your own," he said, sounding like the big brother I never had, someone tak-ing the place of my absent father. "Get up off the floor and let's go sit and have a few. Trust me, you'll have plenty of time to think about how stupid you've been over the past few months about this."

"She left here just as fast as she could. I think she is hurt pretty bad, man," I said, choking back tears.

"Dude, she is fine. You just need to get away from this and give her space and you take space and time to get your mind right about what truly is the best thing to do. Divorce ain't the end of the world, just the end of the world as you two have seen it with one anoth-er," he said wiser than I had ever known or thought of him as being.

"Sometimes that's best. Come on, let's go," he said, giving me a lift up off the floor and pushing me out the door.

I learned another valuable lesson that day.
It was branded on me that love moved everything
within me.   Both the negatives and positives of
my actions had become the same.   I learned potential existed in all the things I had done as
energy I had yet to put into motion, essential-
ly becoming a waste.

I found my ignorance defiled any and every
moment of my life, crushing and exceeding all
my potential.

My most beneficial insights concerning love
had only just begun, sparked during this hor-
rendous moment in time, and the rest is history… ancient history it seems sometimes, but not
all the time, like now…

Daddy's Baby

Writing these words seems simple but true
The day I first laid eyes on you
Now I know the deal
Now life seems so for real
All I want to do is protect your life
Trying hard to minimize strife
Being a parent, what a thrill
Nothing compares to this constant developing skill
If only I could take away all pain, I would
Making all things personal, as if I should...

TL

I was facing divorce again, with the judicial system chasing me down, wanting to crucify me for my crimes. Missy refused to testify, but they still came.

Finally, after months of continuances and absent witnesses, they finally let me go, somewhat. I understood it all, and appreciated it as well, but my mind had been re-arranged and my heart left in shambles. Guilty of trying too hard and causing another pain, I had to heal beyond my loss.

I began counting my blessings.

Albert Einstein once said, "The man who regards life as meaningless is not merely unfortunate, but almost disqualified for life."

Michael was my fortune and I no longer just heard those words, I began to feel them. He inspired me to be more than his dad of deeds, looking to provide his every need. He pushed me to experience and see the glory and magnificence of it all. He opened my eyes to thinking globally, connecting me back to the smallness of our existence. My son, brought the whole lesson of love to completion, eradicating my fear of never being loved, pushing me to understand love by being love to everyone.

I just didn't know how, but I knew I had to find a way.

I did know, more than ever with his arrival, love was something, a substance, an uncontrollable reaction, a movement without grasping, without fear, absent of anything except purity.

I knew that love is…and children epitomize all we could ever summons to describe it, I thought to myself as I read the Dalai Lama's

words in "How To Expand Love," a requirement
for my self-induced anger management class.

"It's in the children," I mumbled, earning
the stares of roller-bladders zooming by as I
sat in the grass Half-Lotus style, calming
myself.

This revelation had been forming for years,
I thought, staring off into the distance as a
few children played tag, chasing each other all
around. A vision of Michael appeared before my
eyes. He was the paramount center in my life,
guiding my actions, my individually controlled
choices, everything. I could hear the universal
connection of love confirm what I already knew,
Michael had come in the name of love for something beyond Missy and I.

Michael made me see the world as individual
selves making choices that affect others in
direct and indirect ways. He brought to me the
real gift of love, revealing to me the true
nature of god, the power of living and the
truth of self-development, brought on by the
very essence of others like and unlike myself.

No greater love compares to the love I received, not only from my child, my gift, but
moreover from those all around me.

He made me see.

I learned love is energy, with the power to
affect many.

He made me feel.

"Trap it away," I heard love say clearly
for the first time, "and an uncomfortable drape
falls over the scene. Open yourself up and the
scene is filled with wonderment, questions,
fascinations, appreciation, acceptance, relaxed
dilemmas, and peace."

He made me aspire.

I yearned to explore these newfound revela-
tions on a permanent basis, but I knew I would
never have the opportunity to make things bet-

ter between Missy and I, and for the first time in the five years we were together, I felt certain "us" no longer existed.

So, I tried to drown my longings in other meaningful things, anything that could use my attention.

I began working 30 to 40 hours a week helping disabled veterans realize their dreams of starting anew after years of searching aimlessly for a reconnect to the real world, begging to escape the demons of their military service. I knew their pain.

I felt if I could help someone break through their barriers and achieve success, my life would feel worth the time and space it took up, since I, hadn't a clue how or why I was continuing on through school, or where I would land afterward. I was on autopilot, not caring much for what would happen. I felt I needed something to give, something to make me feel and know I was alive.

Then she came walking through the door while I was at work one day.

"May I help you?" I asked, immediately caught up in her warm smile and inviting aura, her milky skin shimmering in the badly lit veteran's center.

My very first thoughts about the woman weren't filled with romantic bliss and times of frolicking in a field of flowers. They were flooded with wanting to know the truth and reality behind the idea of love, between man and woman. I felt she knew or could at least help me right myself on my journey. I was roaring with passion, spurring me toward gathering the courage to seek answers to my questions.

"Hello, how are you?" she replied, jolting me from my reveling.

"I'm doing well. What can we do for you?" I asked, trying not to reveal my thoughts, not quite sure how she would perceive me.

"I had an appointment today...do I know you from somewhere? It seems as if we have met before," she said.

"You know, I was thinking the exact same thing," I said, extending my hand out toward her, taking the opportunity to divert her away from deciphering my thoughts. "Tony. It is a sincere pleasure to meet again," I said with a little chuckle bringing a bountiful smile to her face.

"Likewise, I am Sharonn, and I do believe we have, maybe not as ourselves though," she said with a wink.

I could hardly contain myself.

"May I have my hand back now, Mr. Tony?" she said gleefully.

"Oh, damn. My fault. It became second nature there for a while, sorry. Well, let me inform our counselor you're here. Make yourself comfortable and someone will be with you in a little while. By the way, we must talk further, I hope you do realize that?" I said, making an aggressive move, but one I knew needed to be made. I felt my spirit relax from my braveness.

"Definitely. Give me your number and we can go from there."

I knew taking this step allowed me to flow like water effortlessly toward the truth about love. I knew I was taking the first steps toward loving with no limits beyond myself.

Sharonn began helping me shape my cravings and desire to understand existing, beyond merely taking up space for a specific period of time. She helped me form ideas I had never considered before.

"Living means loving," she said, "something we all aspire to do, the reason for love and our lives."

She helped me focus on the beauty of loving anyhow; she placed my focus firmly on Michael... not on the situation he formed from.

Love was simple, inspired by a child, and pure.

She was my first true female friend

I learned the journey was what mattered, not my choices. My choices lead to consequences, questions and more choices, and it was through this tunnel that my journey took shape, and appreciation, admiration, exploration, fascination, wonderment, all the facets of love began taking shape, flowing through me, out to others.

"Sharonn, you know, there is something I don't understand. People say they are connected, but what the hell is that? What does it mean? I've tried it, you've tried it, we've all tried it, and for some reason, it turns out meaning nothing. Is it just a vision, and if so, is it supposed to inspire peace? 'Cause if so, I'm confused and hurting here on this planet, and I just don't get it," I blabbed one day as we were preparing to go running through a nature preserve and enjoy the coolness of the afternoon and the smells signifying the coming of Spring.

"Chuck," she said, calling me by the name she gave me, since I asked lots of questions like the *Peanuts* character, Charlie Brown, "you talk too much." She giggled at my facial response to her blatant words.

"Just look and listen, and all of your questions will be answered without the loss of your air," she said, gleefully pushing me with her words, taking off running down a path headed through a bundle of tightly condensed trees.

"Come on," she called back to me.

After I caught up with her, we ran together in silence for a while, winding along through the trees as they followed the bend of the Illinois River. I forgot all about the throb of my now arthritic knee and enjoyed the beauty of the moment, caught up in the peace of being free. We stopped and sat looking out over the river at the sun glistening, projecting the brilliance of its colors as it set below the waters dark blues, tranquillized by the rippling sounds lulling us.

"You know, Chuck, in due time love always finds a way. I know you know that. It's only through hard times when it doesn't seem to matter anyway. You just can't be afraid to live. And stop worrying so much about making others feel bad; they're human; they want to feel. As long as you're not intentionally causing someone else pain, you have to continue marching with your eyes wide shut. Love is long-suffering, free-flowing and revealing. You can't be afraid of it," she said.

"Yeah, I can see that. I can see that…"

"Well, there's your peace," she said, showing a smile that warmed the moment as much as the setting sun.

About the Author

Born to humble beginnings in Columbus, Georgia on May 19, 1974, TL Darwin spent the greater part of his childhood roaming the fields of rural Georgia before moving to the DC area for a few years prior to joining the Marine Corps. Wherever he has lived, he has spent a lifetime learning and loving, teaching and being taught. He calls the Windy City home now, but through a lot of trial and error and several moves around the world, he has found his real home is in his heart and in the hearts of those he loves. He has written several works of poetry and hopes to continue to find time to expand his writings and to explore his artistic passions.

www.ingramcontent.com/pod-product-compliance
Lightning Source LLC
Chambersburg PA
CBHW020431180626
46812CB00003B/1184